"Okay, I was a bad boy," Dylan said gruffly.

"But after last night's conversation, how do you expect me to stay away?"

Before she could respond, he lowered his head. The first brush of his lips against hers sent an electric current through him just as he expected it would. His entire body tense with restraint, he slanted his mouth across hers and imbibed.

Raising his head, he gazed into her bright eyes. "At least that's out of the way."

"Oh, Dylan, this is such a mistake."

"The tension was starting to hurt everything else," Dylan explained smoothly.

"So," E.D. asked, "we move on to the 'what could it hurt?' temptation?"

"Eva Danielle," he explained, "temptation is a given around you."

Dear Reader,

My interest in this story began as I watched two years of judicial hearings as the latest U.S. Supreme Court justices were being considered in the nation's capital. I felt sympathy for their road traveled, the invasion of privacy for them and their families, and how all of this was compounded as congressional and senatorial elections loomed.

Then days before my deadline, my husband of thirty-one years died of a sudden pulmonary embolism. In that instant, I felt that nothing—not politics, let alone stories of star-crossed love—would ever matter to me again.

Grief doesn't lift by mere will, and the moon often works against the tides to add confusion and despair. But ultimately the realities of life and necessity sink in. It struck me quite clearly that the book I was supposed to write wasn't simply about a woman, law and the loss of a marriage—for better or worse—but life and changes when they are least expected, no matter who you are.

I can't begin to explain the foreshadowing, the messages and understanding I have received during this journey that make this work more poignant for me than anything I've written. For the present, let me just say this learning curve is ongoing and I'm doing my best to respect and embrace it.

Thank you, readers, for your patience, and to my gracious editor Gail Chasan and agent Ethan Ellenberg.

Please enjoy E.D. and Dylan's story. They proved stalwart and durable friends.

Always, thank you for reading. You don't know how we need you.

Warm regards,

Helen

A MAN TO COUNT ON

HELEN R. MYERS

SPECIAL EDITION®

Published by Silhouette Books

America's Publisher of Contemporary Romance

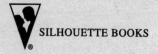

SILHOUETTE BOOKS

ISBN-13: 978-0-373-24830-8
ISBN-10:   0-373-24830-X

A MAN TO COUNT ON

Visit Silhouette Books at www.eHarlequin.com

Printed in U.S.A.

Books by Helen R. Myers

HELEN R. MYERS,

a collector of two- and four-legged strays, lives deep in the Piney Woods of East Texas. She cites cello music and bonsai gardening as favorite relaxation pastimes, and still edits in her sleep—an accident, learned while writing her first book. The bestselling author of diverse themes and focus, she is a three-time RITA® Award nominee, winning for *Navarrone* in 1993.

For my Robert
So many miss you
Me most of all

Prologue

"Congratulations, Judge. I'm so proud and excited for you."

"Thank you, Paulie." Stopping just outside his Austin chambers, Texas Court of Appeals Judge Dylan Justiss smiled fondly at his longtime secretary, Pauline Lawrence. He wasn't surprised she had got wind that the governor himself had encouraged him to file and run in the autumn election to fill a vacancy on one of the state's two highest courts, the Court of Criminal Appeals. If elected, he would replace Thea York, who'd been named to a federal position in Washington, D.C. "But I'll resist upgrading my jogging shoes, until I see who the competition is."

"Once word gets out that you're a candidate, I'll bet you'll be unopposed," Paulie gushed. "Everyone admires and respects you."

"Well, just for that bit of flattery, if you'd like to leave now, I'll sign whatever is on my desk and lock it in yours. I'm going to wait and watch the five o'clock news here before I head home."

The silver-haired woman sporting a flattering wedge beamed at him like an adoring parent. "You're always so thoughtful. How on earth you remembered tonight is my eldest grandson's district play-off game and that he's pitching is beyond me."

Unzipping his black robe, Dylan nodded to one of the photographs on her desk. "Must be the Post-it notes stuck all around the frame of his picture. Let me know how he does."

Enjoying her chuckle, Dylan continued into his suite, quickly rid himself of the robe, and reached for the TV remote. Considering the pace of state, never mind world events, he didn't expect his news to be covered at all, but he wanted to be prepared for anything. Most of the time, judges were invisible beings who were credited, or blamed, by a choice few for decisions that could have widespread and lasting results. However, while in his current position, he presided over one of fourteen courts; if elected in the fall, he would join an elite nine. Anytime change incorporated elevation, he approached it with as much caution as he did respect.

At forty-two, Dylan thought he'd had a good run so far. Great mentors, a phenomenal stretch of pretty smooth sailing regarding cases on his docket, as well as bipartisan support, all of which had allowed him a steady rise up the career ladder. His setbacks had been few and personal—the worst was the death of his wife and best friend, Brenda, eleven months ago after a long illness.

What about a missed, possibly great love?

It was best not to go there.

Then *First News at Five* came on to mock that cautionary thought.

"Good evening, I'm Ross Kendrick. Our top story tonight involves the shocking revelation made by the husband of prominent Deputy District Attorney E. D. Martel. Tonight KTXA can confirm that Trey Sessions has filed for divorce from Ms. Martel, the darling of the D.A.'s office, often called the Black Widow for her consistency in winning the death-penalty verdict. Her latest victory is Ed Guy, convicted only minutes ago for the rape and murder of UT–Austin coed Misty Carthage.

"*KTXA News* has also learned that Sessions has obtained a restraining order to keep Martel from their two children, ages eleven and seventeen, claiming negligence and endangerment of a minor. While we haven't been able to confirm the allegations behind these two career-shattering moves, this also could spell trouble for District Attorney Emmett Garner—his party's likely candidate in the next gubernatorial election—since Martel is said to be his handpicked successor. So far neither D.A. Garner nor Ms. Martel have been available for comment."

And who could blame them? Dylan fumed. Damn. Damn Sessions's useless hide. If anyone was guilty of neglect, Dylan would bet it was E.D.'s house-pet of a husband. What on earth had happened?

While co-anchor Lynly Drew went on to a report about an armed robbery in an Austin hotel parking garage, Dylan dealt with E.D.'s shocking news. He knew—at least he'd heard rumors—that there might be problems in her marriage and that she had been putting a good face on a difficult situation for some time. Whatever househusband Trey thought he'd come upon to make himself less indebted to E.D., it sure as hell couldn't have been her parental neglect. As for endangerment, Dylan would bet a year's salary that allegation was nonsense, too. She would and did do everything and anything it took to give her daughter and son a stable home life. Dylan considered himself proof of that.

He rubbed his face and struggled to keep his thoughts in check. The strength of his impulse to reach for the phone jarred him. They hadn't said more than a few dozen words to each other since Brenda's memorial service last June, and then he couldn't deny being relieved that she'd barely looked him in the eye for fear of what his own gaze might have exposed. Nevertheless, he could remember the poignant encounter down to the second; how she'd first squeezed his hand, how without thinking he'd turned that into a hug and whispered so softly that only she could hear, *"Eva Danielle."* He need only to close his eyes to recall the warmth and softness of her skin, the silk that was her hair, the subtle scent of lily of the valley that always whispered of her presence. The memory continued to haunt him and his insides ached with the deepest hunger pang.

Eva Danielle.

How she hated for anyone to use her given name; his

tightened lips couldn't help but twitch into a brief smile. Too romantic for an attorney, she'd claimed in interviews. She'd once confided to him that she'd been cringing over it since the fifth grade when she'd first become fascinated with law. Eventually, she refused to answer to it, especially after she'd begun to hear people predicting her future as a debutante or some version of trophy wife instead of a determined prosecuting attorney. That charming disclosure had occurred at the University of Texas when she'd been his student escort at an evening lecture he'd been giving there. She had been a senior and he only a few years out of Baylor Law School, but already touted as a rising star in the profession.

A year later they'd met again...on his wedding day, when she'd appeared as the date of one of his groomsmen, Cole Bryce. That had been the oddest of ego blows, although he'd known instinctively there was nothing but affection between them. Regardless, when in six months she'd invited Dylan to her wedding to Sessions, he couldn't bring himself to go.

E. D. Martel—the beautiful, brainy blonde, sharper than many in her field, the woman as devoted to her family as she was to her work—a bad mother? Sure, and the president was a flag burner.

Having tormented himself enough, Dylan reached for his desk phone, hesitated, then snatched up his personal cellular model.

Chapter One

The moment the judge leveled his gavel and announced, "Court is dismissed," E. D. Martel began shaking. Act One, Scene Two accomplished, but she didn't give herself good odds for making it through the next one, let alone the rest of the day.

"We've received word there's a growing swarm of reporters outside, Ms. Martel," her associate and junior counsel Bruce Littner said near her ear. "Some are unfamiliar to me and probably from out of town. I don't know that we can assume they're here for this verdict. You want me to ask the bailiff for a sheriff's deputy to escort you out of here through a back exit?"

More than that, she wanted to wake up in her bed and realize the last several hours had been a bad dream; but she knew better than to accept any protection from the press. There was no denying she was breathless from shock, hurt to the point of wanting to dive into the ladies' room and sob, and angry enough to show Trey what a receding hairline *really* looked like. None of that was an option, though, as Bruce was right; this extra media attention was personal business. Hers. Any outward sign of distress or resentment on her part would serve her, Emmett and the office badly.

With a veteran's ability to press her lips into a semblance of a smile, she touched the concerned young lawyer's shoulder, hating that his biggest professional moment to date ultimately would be reduced to trash. "With your help, I think we can manage. If you'd be so good as to accompany me," she told him, "I'll make the usual 'justice has been served' statement and then, as the give-us-gossip queries begin, excuse us."

The brown-eyed blonde, who could have passed for her kid brother if she'd had one, nodded with emphasis. "You've got it, Ms. Martel. And if any of them get pushy, don't worry. I was a champion wrestler in high school and college. Nobody's going to muscle us."

He was as sweet in his concern as he was thorough in his work. She made a mental note to mention his value to their boss, D.A. Emmett Garner. Who could say—with her luck, he'd be replacing her before Christmas. "Make that E.D. You've earned it. As for trouble, I suspect the only threat we need to worry about is a chipped tooth from having a microphone jammed into our faces."

As she slipped the strap of her purse over her shoulder and reached for her briefcase, she wondered at her calm voice and hoped that the sweat starting to trickle down her back and between her breasts didn't bleed through her red suit. She traditionally wore this suit with the double-breasted gold buttons on final arguments day, when murder one was on the table, to keep the jury's attention. She opted for a black one on the day she expected a jury verdict, to signify her awareness that another life had been lost, and that everyone loses in a conviction.

Only today the jury hadn't taken two hours to reach their decision.

It was just as well, she reasoned. The red could substitute as her internal grieving for what her children must be going through.

So help me, Trey, you will pay for this.

Operating on reflexes that she'd honed from almost sixteen years with the district attorney's office, E.D. accepted the teary thanks, emotional hugs and powerful handshakes from poor Misty Carthage's family and friends. That barely slowed her path toward the double doors, beyond which cameras would click madly and video cameras would catch every nuance. Knowing she had seconds before the full circus started, she told Bruce, "When you get out of here, take that patient girl of yours out for a terrific dinner. If you want to try Bruno's, use my name and have them charge it to my account. One of us deserves a good meal out of this."

Usually someone with above-average reflexes, the attorney had to reach twice for the door handle. "Uh…thanks. You're sure?"

E.D. blocked thoughts of what Trey had done with

their joint accounts while she'd been tied up in court. "Absolutely. Now let's get this done."

Bruce opened the door to a barrage of people and electronics. From the bulwark poured eager and strident appeals.

"Are you pleased at putting another defendant on death row, Ms. Martel?"

"E.D., is it true your husband has locked you out of your own home?"

"Did you know the photos you approved would end up on the Internet?"

"The word is that *Playboy* is offering you a million for a mother-daughter layout. Gonna take it?"

Wishing she could broadside smug Josh Perle with her briefcase, E.D. paused and began, "Thank you for your interest in Misty Carthage's devastating case. The state of Texas is grateful that justice has been served once again and that other studious coeds, the Austin community as a whole, will be safer—at least from the likes of Ed Guy."

"With this being May, you'll soon have two condemned men facing execution," another reporter she didn't recognize called from the back. "New DNA tests are being requested by their attorneys. What's your reaction to that?"

"It's their right, of course. That said, the Sandman did not beat Debra Conyers to death in her bed, her husband did, despite his recant after excessive publicity attracted a high-profile defense team to his case. As for Counselor Baltow's claim regarding *his* client, science has already shown the state will not be putting an innocent person to death and I expect that new appeal will be denied, as well. Thank you for your time."

After a speaking glance to Bruce, she started down the hall. Undaunted, several reporters matched her stride.

"Would you make a statement about Mr. Martel's decision to sue you for divorce and get a restraining order, Ms. Martel?"

"No." But E.D. wished Trey could hear himself being referred to by her maiden name. The reporter had to be new.

"Have you talked to your daughter or son?" someone else asked in a sharper voice.

Caught off guard, she ignored the question due to the sudden boulder lodging in her throat. Thankfully, Bruce forced his way forward and stretched out his arm to deter the persistent.

"Back off! You have your statement."

Three minutes later she reached her office, rejecting Bruce's offer to escort her the rest of the way. She'd expressed her gratitude again and urged him toward the parking garage. Now she drew in a long, deep breath knowing she wouldn't get off so easy. The sound reminded her of a rattling shutter in a storm.

Don't.

As her throat began to hurt anew, she tried to ease that by swallowing several times. She had no time for tears, forget outright panic. But vulnerability was compounding on itself. Sure, for the moment she had a job where she would be defended in any public forum. All it would take to end that, though, was a few more crass comments by Trey, Dani in hysterics…and the photos showing up in more and more places. Then, whether it was fair or not, E.D. would be asked for her resignation, left as raw meat to the voracious media hounds.

One thing at a time. Get through here, and then figure out where you'll sleep tonight.

She honestly didn't have a clue. By the first break in court today, Trey had left a message on her cell phone warning her not to return to the house because he'd had the locks changed so she wouldn't be able to get inside. Supposedly, her luggage was waiting for her in her office. Not only hadn't the bastard had the decency to let her pack her own things, he was subjecting her to the humiliation of the whole office seeing evidence that she was being ejected from her own home—for reasons as bizarre as they were infuriating.

As E.D. walked the long halls, she again tried to call her seventeen-year-old daughter, Dani—but without success. Mac, her eleven-year-old son, didn't answer his phone, either. Trey must have had some input there. As bad as Dani's situation was—and she had yet to get to the bottom of it—surely he hadn't succeeded in convincing her son that she was in any way responsible?

Walking through the halls, she willed her expression to remain blank and only murmured, "Thanks," to the half-dozen people who were still there working on their own cases, looking up to congratulate her. She'd encouraged her secretary, Nita, not to wait on her—a good thing because as she opened the door to her office, the

sight of her three red suitcases had her slumping against
the door, her vision blurring from tears.

Remember where you are.

Real help came as her phone started vibrating. Hoping it was Mac or Dani, she straightened and reached
into her pocket. When she checked the caller ID screen,
she couldn't believe her eyes.

Dylan Justiss!

Why she continued to keep his number on her
personal phone she couldn't say—or didn't want to
admit. But realizing that she was a button click away
from hearing his strong, reassuring voice had her
insides fluttering in excitement.

Someone discreetly coughed behind her.

Pivoting, she saw a suave-looking, mature man, his
hair barely a shade lighter than his steel-gray eyes and
suit. "Sir."

"Congratulations, E.D.," Travis County District
Attorney Emmett Garner said with a regal nod. "You've
done me proud again."

"Thank you. Though considering the amount of
DNA evidence, I think a final-year law student could
have handled this case." Pocketing her phone, she
gestured. "Care to come in?"

Apparently, he did, and while he eyed the luggage,
it was noteworthy that he made no comment. Instead,
he shut the door, leaned back against it, and assumed a
deceptively casual pose of folded arms and crossed
ankles. Cary Grant never did it better. E.D. had once read
that while in college, Emmett had done Shakespeare
onstage, earning reviews that could have launched a

stage career if he'd wanted it. Aside from his smooth, sophisticated features, his precise diction and lack of any Western twang seemed to support that; however, his performance hall had become a Texas courtroom, and he'd tried some of the most important cases in the state's history, winning the majority soundly.

"I hope you didn't stay late because of me?" E.D. asked, preferring to get this over with rather than deal with a prolonged silence. Reaching her desk, she set her bag and briefcase onto it and met his shrewd scrutiny straightforward.

"Because of and *for* these few words, my dear. Delayed an engagement after I heard the verdict," he intoned. "I wanted an opportunity to salute *Le Martel* and see for my own eyes how, under the circumstances, the day's events affected my faithful soldier. Elegant, but a gladiator still," he added with a satisfied gleam in his eyes. "You reassure me."

Meaning he'd heard the worst and had questions about his "best and brightest" being in deep domestic trouble. E.D. admired and often liked Emmett, but she had no illusions about how fast he would give the thumbs-down signal to feed her to the two-legged lions if she polluted his precious department and crippled his political future.

"You trained your protégée well, sir. I, too, would like to recognize someone—my assistant, Bruce Littner. He deserves a letter in his file for his part in this verdict."

"See that it's done. At the rate we wear out staff, it's

always good to remember to stroke the young talent, and I've long admired your nose for potential stars."

"Thank you."

Without breaking eye contact, Emmett tilted his head toward the luggage. "I'm not going to meddle, unless you feel the need for a confidant…and I think that same fine mind is far too intelligent to want me to be one."

Velvety words barely cloaking a steel-hard warning had the desired effect on E.D. This wasn't the first time she had heard them, although it was the first since rising so high in the department. "You flatter me, sir. But I plan to continue separating work and family.

"This should be simply a divorce case at worst," she continued, holding his penetrating gaze. If she'd had a choice, she would as soon take her chances with a great white shark. "As for the T.R.O., I'm afraid there's nothing I can do tonight about the media's carnivorous interest in the temporary restraining order. However, I'll seek injunctive relief first thing tomorrow morning. In the meantime, you can be assured I signed no authorization whatsoever for my daughter to model, and would certainly never approve of *those* kind of photographs.

"Danielle is barely seventeen." She lowered her voice to a near whisper to guarantee his focus. "As a mother, my heart is aching for my daughter's humiliation. As an attorney, I'm furious that yet another predator has apparently taken advantage of a minor and I plan to make him—or whomever is responsible—rue the day they hatched this plan."

Despite her quiet dignity, Emmett looked only marginally reassured. "You have my deepest sympathies and support, as well as the resources of this office to prosecute what I'm hearing from you is a criminal act. But…I would prefer it not to be played out on the front pages of the newspapers and on TV. At least not now. I think you agree with me that this would be in no one's best interests?"

E.D. clasped her hands behind her back to keep him from seeing her fist them. *No one,* meaning Emmett Garner. She could see the gears in his mind working and knew that he was concerned about a "guilt by association" implication. At fifty-eight, he was in prime professional and political condition to take the governor's seat in the next election. It was critical for him to leave the D.A.'s office on a high note. E.D. had no intention of making a public show of her daughter's naiveté or foolishness—whichever this proved to be—but she would be damned if Emmett's ambitions cost her child legal justice.

"Protecting the privacy of a minor is my first and greatest concern," she said coolly.

Ever the image of self-containment, Emmett checked his watch. "Initially, this is bound to impact your schedule."

The nerve of the man, she fumed in silence. E.D. had successfully juggled a tough schedule through two pregnancies, *and* had returned to work early each time. As an aspiring novelist, Trey had been eager to stay at home with the babies. Oh, she thought with a new sinking feeling, how she had played into her husband's hands.

"There. That's exactly why I came to see you," Emmett snapped, pointing a professionally manicured finger at her. "There's self-doubt on your face. Since when does E. D. Martel let anyone see anything less than resolve?"

Since her I'm-writing-the-great-American-novel spouse pulled something she had yet to fully comprehend. Since their daughter had walked, tripped or otherwise been lured neck-deep into a disaster that could haunt her the rest of her life. Dani couldn't begin to know the breadth and width of what she'd done, but E.D. dealt with such things 24/7.

Drawing a steadying breath, she offered, "This is Wednesday, and as you know I have the Horvath case starting Monday, which will bring the office as much attention, if not more, than the Guy case did. If I haven't shown you that I'm up to your standards by the end of opening remarks, replace me."

E.D. had no idea if her challenge was all bravado, let alone sensible.

What she was convinced of was that she hadn't spent the last thirty-eight years of her life building to this, only to chicken out even before she fully understood what she was dealing with.

Emmett studied her another moment and then pushed himself away from the door. "I'm glad that we understand each other. See you at seven-thirty for the regular java and jockeying session."

As he let himself out, E.D. responded to the sudden weakness in her legs and lowered herself to sit on the edge of her desk. She had no illusions as to what he

meant by the word *understand:* If she didn't lead the
D.A.'s team in the Horvath case—and win—her future
here was over. It didn't matter that it would require two
clerks to assist her and Bruce in the face-off with Lester
Horvath's pricey defense team. Somehow she would
still have to figure out a way to reason with Trey, as well
as help the children. Where would she find the extra
hours in her already crammed days, let alone the energy
to use them wisely?

A knock on her door had E.D. starting. Had Emmett
changed his mind and decided he wanted her off the
case after all?

"Come in."

A young man poked his head inside. "Ms. Martel?"

"Yes." A courier, she thought with relief, noting his
cyclist's helmet tucked under his arm.

"I have an express for you."

Praying it wasn't another *present* from Trey, E.D.
accepted the small padded packet, only to stare at the
sender's bold initials. *D.J.* Incredible! So the call wasn't
an accident. But what was Dylan doing and could she
afford to satisfy her curiosity?

For a moment she was tempted to reject the delivery;
her instincts told her it was the wise thing to do. The
use of just his initials was proof that this was personal
and for her eyes only. Dylan needed a paper trail to her
right now about as much as Emmett wanted one; after
all, she'd heard the latest rumor about Dylan filing for
the upcoming election.

Feeling caught in some game where she didn't know
the goal let alone the rules, E.D. yielded to temptation

and signed the appropriate line on the delivery record. Plucking out a folded bill from the side compartment of her purse, she handed it over along with the clipboard. "Thank you."

"Thank *you,* ma'am."

As she waited for the gangly, spandex-dressed youth to leave, her thoughts circled around the ludicrous concern that her signature didn't resemble her usual confident flourish and that her hands refused to stop trembling. But as soon as she heard the door click closed, she tore at the padded envelope.

He had to have seen the news this morning, she thought as she pulled out the smaller envelope inside. Maybe he—her breath caught as she felt something hard inside.

Oh, no!

He'd been bold. Mad. So out of character for steady, live-by-the-rules Dylan.

E.D. tore the smaller envelope and dropped the contents into her cupped left palm. As she'd surmised, a shiny brass key landed there. She closed her fingers around it and pressed her fist to her pounding heart.

You dear man. You crazy, idealistic man.

Shaking her head, she checked the envelope to see if he'd included a message. A brief note had been handwritten on a blank sheet of notepad paper.

You know what this goes to. Use it.

Scrawled below were four numbers. As the past rushed forward to replay itself before her eyes, E.D. shook her head and debated over the options that unfolded before her. There was no mistaking that she'd been reminded of the rest of his cell-phone number; she didn't need to check her directory to confirm that. The question was should she respond?

She had to. Such a gesture—regardless of his motives—made some response mandatory. But as she retrieved her phone out of her pocket, she didn't deceive herself; the pounding in her ears was less about what common sense demanded she say than eagerness to hear his voice again. *That* shamed the woman who was a mother and, until today, a damned faithful and caring wife.

Navigating to the correct memory code, E.D. punched the call button. After only half a ring, she heard the voice that embraced and reassured like no other.

"I was beginning to give up hope. What else can I do?"

The part of her that had been increasingly ignored and becoming repressed whispered, "*Ah*." Dylan's voice had always reminded her of profound things: the baritone bell ending a monastery prayer, the timely discovery of a quilt during a hard winter freeze. The professional man inspired equally stirring and lasting feelings in people. He stood statue tall and was built as physically well as he was mentally solid, more than capable of enduring strong political winds and ethical challenges. It was difficult to look into his ink-blue eyes and not be overwhelmed; framed by a strong-boned face, they radiated wisdom, wit and a patience honed from years of watching and listening. E.D. missed that face, that voice, and more, their strange, indefinable friendship.

Wondering if his pitch-brown hair was tumbling over his broad brow by now from hours bent over files and law books, she managed a smile, wistful though it was. "You shouldn't have done anything in the first place."

"I've already worked through that argument myself and found it wanting."

She cupped the phone as though it were his cheek. "I think you let sympathy override sensibility. As generous as the gesture is, it's impossible."

"Why? You need to sleep, a quiet place to think."

When Trey had first hit her with his accusations and threats last night, E.D.'s impulse had been to call Dylan—not for aid, but advice. If anyone could think of something that could be done to stop this insanity before it mushroomed into a blinding, noxious cloud that permanently damaged her children, she'd suspected he would. However, just as quickly, she'd reasoned she would be every bit as poisonous to Dylan. Any contact could potentially stain a brilliant career that seemed to be about to take off to new heights; and so she'd resisted.

"I don't know what to say." She studied the key to the comfy but rustic cabin west of the city, about forty minutes into the hill country. "I'm grateful, of course, but…this is so embarrassing."

"If anyone should be embarrassed it's your—" Dylan's sigh spoke of frustration "—it wasn't my intention to make you feel awkward. After I saw the report on TV, I could only imagine what hell this has been for you. How's your daughter?"

"I wish I could tell you. I haven't been able to reach either of the kids."

"And you?"

"I've had excellent training at hanging on by my fingernails."

"You can't ask me to stand by and do nothing."

No, not the man whose last name perfectly described him; Dylan Justiss had been born to serve the law. However, this time he'd picked the wrong battle.

"You're wonderful." She hoped her sincerity carried through in those two simple words. "But that doesn't change that I can't let you do this."

"So you're going to a hotel and face curious stares from staff when they deliver room service? Reporters paying for a heads-up call that you're leaving, or details about where you're going and with whom?"

He had her there. She was dreading that possibility, so much so that she'd considered driving out of town to find a sanctuary. Trey had already blocked her from their joint checking account and put a freeze on everything else they held jointly, but she had enough personal resources to survive for a while without having to borrow from the firm or friends. The added lure of Dylan's offer was that his retreat would make her truly invisible…if the arrangement could be kept secret.

"It's been years since I've driven out there, and it would be perfect, except for—"

"I know we're both being careful not to say too much because we're not on secure lines," Dylan replied. "All I want to do is assure you, it is private and exactly what you need. My caretaker will know to expect you and unless you ask for help, you'll be left alone."

He'd put serious thought into this and that added to E.D.'s torment. Despite her concern for security, she needed to take a risk and make him see what an error he could be making. "This is supposed to be the happiest professional day of your life—and I am so pleased and proud for you—but look at what you're doing. Why would you risk your future by having any contact with me? If this gets out, don't you realize what conclusions people will draw?"

The sigh that came over the line sent her heart sinking as deeply as when she'd first heard of Dani's crisis. So he *was* only being a gentleman and would let her talk him out of this. Well, she appreciated the gesture nonetheless. No one else had stepped forward so gallantly.

After a considerable silence Dylan opined, "And here I thought you knew me better than that."

Could she have underrated him that much? E.D. pressed her fingers to her lips to fight back a building sob. "The fact is I don't claim to know anyone anymore," she forced herself to admit.

"Oh, I think *we* know each other so well, it's scaring you," he countered. "Use the key or I'll come get you myself."

Chapter Two

Use the key...

It should have been impossible for E.D. to smile, but she did, several times on her drive to Dylan's personal refuge. First because he'd pulled the kind of threat that should only be successful on puppies and kids under the age of five. When she was a child, her family had had a rebellious, independent pup that had never obeyed the simplest command until he'd heard her father's warning, "Don't make me come get you." And then the leggy critter would charge for the stairs as if a T-bone was on the other side of the kitchen door. Dylan couldn't possibly know that story, but he'd used the technique with her father's intonation.

Next she smiled appreciating the man's tenderness and compassion. What a pity that she couldn't extol his goodness publicly. Regardless of what lay down the road, she would cherish his friendship and generosity.

Dylan's ranch—although he was the last to call it that due to its modest size by Texas standards—was five hundred–plus acres in the Hill Country, property that he'd inherited from his parents after their untimely death while on vacation. He kept it because he wisely knew the most patrolled property in Austin couldn't assure him the serenity and privacy these rolling hills of the rough prairie did. E.D. suspected that Dylan also kept it because a part of him clung to a dream never voiced to anyone but himself.

It took close to an hour to get there, her fault thanks to a wrong turn that cost her extra time. At the electronic gate, she spent another minute figuring out the keypad code. Dylan hadn't provided it, which told her that he knew she could figure it out—and wanted her to. Suddenly reminded of the note with the last four digits of his phone number and his appreciation for puzzles, she tried it two different ways without success, then thought of "gate" and split, *then* inverted the two sets of numbers…and the real gate opened.

Shaking her head at his wit, as much as his determination not to allow her to get buried in fear and self-pity, she drove in. Mesquite, cedar and rock outcroppings protected the view of the house from the main road. Originally a one-bedroom log cabin, the building had been renovated to add on another bedroom, bathroom and a dream kitchen. E.D. remembered the layout only slightly from the wedding, but knew one thing for certain—she wouldn't be sleeping in the bed where Dylan and Brenda had spent their honeymoon. That would finish denying her a wink of rest. One of the couches would serve her fine for this short stay.

As she pulled up to the house, she saw the lights on and a Jeep in front. A wiry-built man in his early forties pushed himself up from one of the large cypress rockers on the porch and stepped out to greet her. He wore a worn straw hat and denim work clothes, and politely removed the hat.

"Ms. Martel?"

How not surprising, E.D. thought. Dylan had obviously instructed his foreman how to address her. "E.D., please," she said extending her hand. "You're…?"

"Coats, ma'am. Chris Coats." After the handshake, he pointed west of the house. "My cabin is down by the creek about a quarter of a mile. Press one on the phone's memory dial or use the walkie-talkie if you need me. You'll find your radio by the bed stand. If you're planning to walk around outside after dark, I'd appreciate you letting me know. We have our share of snakes and varmints, you know."

"I think I can safely assure you that I won't test my luck."

He nodded approvingly. "The fridge is freshly stocked and all utilities and linens have been checked. Is there anything else I can do, ma'am? Did you have dinner? My cooking won't keep you up all night if you have a taste for a steak or an omelet."

E.D. smiled. She felt comfortable with this what-you-see-is-what-you-get throwback to a fast-fading era, but suspected he'd already put in a long day with the stock and repairing fences, or whatever his job description included. "You're kind, but I suspect it's already been a long day for you, and I—" she'd almost said *I lost my appetite before I went to bed last night.* Quickly editing herself, she continued, "I'll be fine, thank you very much."

"My pleasure, ma'am. Having anticipated that you may be tired, there's a salad, also a stew in the fridge that only needs warming. I'll just get your luggage inside and be on my way."

E.D. waited for him with her shoulder bag and briefcase in hand, wondering what his story was and how long Dylan had entrusted this mystical place to him. On further study she noted that he moved like a man of thirty-five or so, but his weathered features suggested adding some years. Suspecting that as much as he liked it here that life wasn't a free ride, she appreciated Chris all the more for making this so easy for her—at least as easy as an already humiliated woman could feel at this point.

Minutes later, she stood alone in the cabin. It wasn't her familiar two-story Tudor with halls full of family photos, hutches of antique crystal, silver and china, some that she could trace back to great-grandparents. Yes, there were antiques, but of a more primitive Mexican design. Interspersed with large leather couches and chairs, they reflected Dylan's grounded, stable personality well and she could see him everywhere she looked.

Strangely, that left her feeling all the more of a fraud what with her home being predominantly about status and image and less about who she was. Save for her sunroom-breakfast nook, it struck E.D. that the word *home* had become mostly a lie to her. At least in the nook she could corner the kids long enough to share their experiences and ask about anxieties. It was also where her African violets and orchids caught her attention, getting the water and fertilizer they needed to bloom. She shook her head, realizing she'd have been willing to sacrifice the plants if her kids could have thrived more. The den was well lived in, thanks to the kids' study marathons and movie parties. But except for their bedrooms, the rest of the house was all for appearance—the French provincial dining room, the equally formal parlor. As for Trey's office, it was known as No Man's Land to everyone including her, and yet also furnished to give the impression of intellectualism and success. That was the biggest joke considering that all those wooden file cabinets contained were unfinished manuscripts and rejection letters.

As bitterness rose again like bile in her throat, the phone rang.

E.D. glanced around and found the remote on the sofa table. Grabbing it, she saw the caller ID information and smiled. "Yes, I'm here," she said in lieu of a greeting.

"Good. I was beginning to worry."

Aware she was breathing like a sprinter, E.D. pressed a hand to her heart.

"I made a wrong turn and almost ended up in El Paso."

Despite the hilly terrain, a baritone chuckle came back clearly over the wireless connection.

"You'd be thirsty and hungry long before you got there."

No doubt. She dismissed that to communicate her reactions to what he was making available to her. "Oh, my. I'd forgotten how refreshing yet peaceful it was here."

"Sorry that I didn't have time to do anything special."

E.D. supposed he meant flowers. "Your man was here waiting. He's been very kind—and thorough. Thank you."

"You're most welcome. Now that that's out of the way, how are you, really?"

Several people had asked her that, but this was the first time that E.D. felt she could dissolve into a puddle upon hearing the question. She had to swallow hard not to embarrass both of them. "Stunned. Worried. Hurt. Getting angrier by the minute."

"All understandable and probably healthy reactions. I'm particularly supportive of the latter one."

"Unfortunately, it's a luxury I can least afford. He may not let me speak to them, but I need to look into who he's hired to represent her." *He,* meaning Trey. *Her*, meaning her daughter. E.D. knew better than to give out names on yet another open line and suspected from his careful wording that Dylan continued to share her mindset.

"Is there something I can do from this end?" he asked.

Any queries he made would immediately make him vulnerable to public speculation. She had no doubt he could handle that, but could his career at this fragile juncture? "Thank you, but opening your home to me is more than enough."

There was a slight pause on the line, then he said, "Since it's obvious you're not going to rest, I can help you think things through."

E.D. covered her eyes with her left hand. "It's humiliating to know you've heard what you have. I can't bring myself to discuss them with you at this point, even if I had all the truth, which I don't. He won't talk to me, and he's cut me off from my own children. Me! I'm the one who can actually help."

As her voice broke, she compressed her lips and shifted her hand from her eyes to her mouth to help fight back a sob.

For a good while there was only the sound of Dylan breathing on the other end of the connection. Finally, he said with new determination, "There's a fax machine in my office. Why don't you go turn it on?"

"Excuse me?"

"You need an attorney willing to do what you're in no condition to do for yourself. I'm writing down a name and number."

How did she tell him that her finances were complicated right now, that Trey had locked her out of their checking and savings and had changed the passwords on their money market account? She had funds to secure a divorce attorney, but a top gun to go after the scum that was hurting her child? That was a different matter entirely.

Her silence apparently spoke fathoms to Dylan.

"Let me cover whatever retainers you need."

She couldn't believe he would make such an offer, let alone not recognize what a paper trail that would leave. "I'm sorry," she said abruptly, "but I need a minute."

Without giving him an opportunity to protest, she disconnected, and with her insides roiling for the second time today, E.D. sought and found the bathroom and became physically ill. The day's events were taking their toll and the only good news was that her stomach was mostly empty, which made her discomfort thankfully short-lived. Unfortunately, after she washed her face and rinsed her mouth, she was left back where she'd started—gruesomely aware of the long journey ahead, a journey full of traps and pitfalls regardless of the route she chose to take. Like her day job didn't provide plenty of that.

Worried that Dylan would assume the worst and charge over here, she forced herself to key his number. Once again he answered immediately.

"You do know how to keep a guy's attention. Better now?"

He spoke with a suspicious calmness and E.D. had the strongest urge to go to the window to make sure he wasn't parked outside. "Ask me in six months…more likely a year." God have mercy, she thought, please don't let it all take that long. But it probably would— or longer yet—and Dylan's failure to contradict her told her that he believed much the same thing.

"The good news is that often cases like your daughter's have a tendency to settle out of court," he said at last. "As to the other, let's hope his attorney will see what prolonging the divorce would do to the kids."

"We both know what his divorce attorney is thinking," E.D. replied. It had nothing to do with their children's well-being and everything to do with her willingness to pay to keep this out of the press as much as possible. Since both attorney fees would, inevitably, be coming out of her pocket there was no thought of hiring a private judge to assure that. "I'm heading toward the office and the fax machine. That said, as much as I appreciate your input, please know your offer is out of the question."

Not surprisingly, her tone had him pausing again. Finally, he told her, "I'm only keeping my peace because I want you to continue talking to me."

She wanted to. Their profession kept her busy and she knew many people, but trust was hard earned and allegiances too easily bought—and sold. Real friendships were priceless. That didn't mean she didn't feel the need to keep warning him off. "You should have clued me in on your predilection for gut-stomping punishment."

"Takes one to know one."

He had her there, she thought, flipping on the light switch in his office. "All right, moving on then. Give me a second to figure out how this thing works. Wait—we have this model in our office." She turned on the machine. "Assuming you have a separate line for this, go ahead."

After only a half minute the motor hummed to life. A single sheet printed in Dylan's strong handwriting slid into the tray. E.D. narrowed her eyes on the name. "You can't be serious?" *Ivan Priestly.* "He's the Mount Rushmore among attorneys. Good grief, he's as *old* as Rushmore!"

"Don't let that unruly mane of white hair fool you. He's only seventy-two."

"Meaning if he hasn't retired, he's bound to at any minute."

"Correction, he's discriminating about what cases he takes. He's fit for his age and enjoys fishing too much with the grandkids to accept every request that comes along," Dylan informed her. "And trust me, he still gets plenty of them."

"Yet another reason why this isn't a good idea." With defeat looking increasingly probable, E.D.'s tone exposed her plunging spirits. "This sleazy dilemma is going to be a turn-off to someone so esteemed. I need a snake masquerading as a fox, and you're proposing a cross between Moses and Peter Pan."

Dylan laughed. "He's exactly who isn't expected. Though you're right about his bringing gravitas to the table. Between the two of you, whoever ends up the sitting judge for the trial will damned sure check his law before allowing any nonsense from the other side."

She could feel herself blush. "That's undeserved flattery for me. I'll need to wear slacks to court every day for fear my knocking knees will disrupt the sessions. Please—" she barely caught herself from blurting out his name "—you know this is impossible. He'll never say yes."

"You won't know unless you ask him."

"Which I won't do. It would be an indignity, an insult to his reputation."

"Apply that same conviction to yourself. Someone has dared to compromise your dignity by using your child. *Your* reputation demands the best."

E.D. closed her eyes against the wealth of emotions rushing through her. This was why she kept his number in her directory. He was so compassionate and good. He was her ideal on virtually every level.

"Do you trust me?" he asked quietly.

With all of my heart.

But she had no right to think with it. It was her daughter's future she needed to focus on. "Hold on. I'm shutting off the machine." The request was a pitiful feint; however, it bought her the precious seconds she needed. Slumping into the plush leather chair behind his desk, she flung the sheet of paper with Ivan Priestly's phone number onto the spotless blotter.

"I can hear you breathing."

His words couldn't remotely be called chiding, but E.D. hid her face in her hand nonetheless. "You should do yourself a favor and say good night."

"Is that a serious request or more self-derision?"

Was he kidding? She was partly being so hard on herself because she was afraid of when he did hang up and left her alone to deal with her own mind. There were thoughts buried deep behind walls and under thick floors constructed to never allow what he was making her feel or fantasize…those thoughts would want air. Free will.

"If you're going to make me work this hard at

reading your mind," Dylan said, his voice gruff, "I should at least be allowed to see your eyes."

His tender complaint sent a new delicious trembling whispering through her, one she didn't have the energy or desire to repress. Ridiculous, she thought in the next instant. She was a married woman, eyebrow-deep in scandal—besides, surely he had someone, the proverbial *significant other* in his life by now…?

"You can't come out here." She didn't need a mirror to know she looked like death warmed over, the last of her makeup just washed off, her eyes bloodshot from strain as much as from fighting tears the entire day. Dylan would be a dangerous mix of gentle strength and undeniable masculinity. Too tempting.

"All right. Not tonight…if you'll promise to have a hot bath and go to bed. Whether you sleep or not, your body needs to stop," he continued as though sensing her protest coming. "You're too exhausted to reason clearly. You're aware of that, aren't you?"

"Yes."

"Good. We can debate things further tomorrow if you insist, as long as you understand that I am serious about being there for you. Try not to file that away under *D* for *denial*, okay?"

"Getting Mount Rushmore's support could be a coup," she said, feeling a need to give him some ground.

"Who were you considering to handle your divorce? Or do you see the potential for reconciliation?"

E.D. almost choked. "That's not remotely funny."

"Stranger things have happened," he said with no inflection whatsoever.

"Well, it won't here."

The anger in her voice made her wince, but on the heels of that rushed certainty: her marriage had been suffering for a good while. She'd been delaying looking at the possible reasons, aware that inevitably she'd contributed to some of the problems between her and Trey. But his conduct was offsetting any guilt she had been willing to accept.

"Have you heard of Alyx Carmel?" she asked. "She's risen to be one of the best divorce attorneys in the South." And as luck would have it, they'd belonged to the same sorority at UT. E.D. hoped that would help her to negotiate some financial compromises as she worked out her financial bird's nest.

"I've heard of her," Dylan replied. "Didn't she win a tough suit a few months ago for some widow—real estate heiress?"

"Benton versus Benton, that's right. The stepkids were so power hungry they attempted to even dig into assets derived by the stepmother's first husband."

"Unusual. There wasn't a trust? Those are difficult to invade."

"That bottom line fell just below the requirements. And thanks to the new and ferocious generation of legal minds, many previously solid wills are considered breakable."

Dylan sighed. "Dare I hope you don't have to navigate those tricky waters?"

"Who knows what else Trey has up his sleeve? Let's just say that imagining the attorney fees reminds me that I'm in the wrong side of this business."

"Your problem is that you were never a bottom line person, though I must admit it's another thing I admire about you. After you talk to Mount Rushmore, *call me*."

"All right." E.D. wanted him to know one thing. "You're wonderful, you know that?"

Before he could reply she disconnected.

Energized by his support, she reached for her cell phone.

Chapter Three

E.D. waited for the phone to start ringing. Dylan was right; she was the wronged party and she knew of no judge who would look into this situation and not wonder, "Why?"

Almost immediately Trey came on the line with a curt, "You shouldn't be harassing me."

E.D. opened her mouth to define exactly what harassment he deserved, then considered that he might have a recording device handy. Editing herself, she replied, "It's barely past eight, Trey, and you know we have things to discuss. But first I'd like to speak to the kids."

"You know how restraining orders read. You can't."

"How you managed that I don't know, but understand this, you are doing more damage than you can imagine."

"I'm only protecting my daughter and son."

"*Our* children, Trey. And you know damned well I know nothing about this mess with Dani. If anyone should, it's you, since you see her more than I do."

"How long does it take to negligently sign something she shoves under your nose?"

His condescension made her empty stomach burn. "I told you last night that I did nothing of the kind, and when that hack photographer is ordered to produce my signature in court, your apology won't be enough. The fact that you so easily believe him over me is beyond insulting."

"I believe my daughter."

That was what had made her physically sick earlier, the assertion that Dani supposedly claimed E.D. had signed the document. Tonight, she was desperate to determine why her child would say such a thing. "She couldn't possibly have said that."

"Oh, stop pretending. You haven't been a wife or mother in longer than any of us can remember. I had no choice but to conclude you were so preoccupied with your career that you'd approve anything just not to be bothered."

E.D. cringed. She had shortchanged her kids due to her workload. But unlike her kids, Trey had no business judging her. "Has the reason for that crossed your mind? How else are the bills to be paid? We can't both sit at home and languish in a fantasy world."

"Smart move insulting my misfortune."

"Dani is the only victim in this house. No one owes you a writing career. Either you produce something people want to read, or you face reality and get a day job like everyone else. The kids are old enough to manage on their own an hour or two after school. Good grief, with Dani's dance lessons three times a week, she's already under adult supervision."

After a slight pause, Trey taunted, "Want to go for the full strikeout?"

His smug tone was inflaming her long-repressed resentment and E.D. could barely contain herself. If only she'd put her foot down sooner. If only she'd listened to the small voice in her head warning her that if she waited too long, her marriage would be a weight that could sink her in more ways than one. Hindsight was going to prove as bitter a pill as the rest.

Drawing a deep breath, she forced herself to ask calmly, "At least tell me if Dani ate something today?"

"She tried, she couldn't keep anything down."

Her poor baby. "Please call Dr. Warren if things aren't better tomorrow. What about Mac? How's his asthma? He was pretty upset after he heard us last night." E.D. had come home late yet again and at first had assumed all was well and that the kids were in their rooms doing homework or visiting with friends. Within minutes that assumption had been shattered, and by the time Trey had stormed off to bed, it was obvious that all of their lives were changing forever.

His silence brought her attention back to the present. "I'll hold. Please go check on him. *Do it, Trey.*"

After another hesitation, Trey muttered, "Okay."

His acquiescence surprised and worried her. Did this mean he'd not seen Mac for hours and only now remembered him? Their son was the true introvert, a quiet soul who could get lost in his projects and painstaking study forgetting everything including the need to breathe.

"He's fine."

Startled at Trey's abrupt bark, E.D. took a second to regroup. "He has his inhaler? There haven't been any episodes?"

"I said he's fine. Don't start acting like I don't know what I'm doing. Everyone in the neighborhood knows that I've been holding down the fort for years. Now if you'll excuse me—"

"Trey, wait!" E.D. hated the sound of desperation in her voice, but she hadn't nearly covered all that she wanted to. "Just do me the courtesy of answering one or two more questions. *Please*."

"What?" he snapped.

E.D. wrapped her free arm around her waist. The ache there warned her that if she didn't reduce the stress and intense emotions in her life, she would soon be fighting an ulcer. "Has that Web site you mentioned that has Dani's pictures on it been shut down?"

"Uh...I don't know."

What did he mean he didn't know? "Every hour it's up has to be an unbearable humiliation for her, Trey."

"I've been busy!"

Doing what? Figuring his options after he finished taking her to the cleaners? "What do the police say? Have you hired someone to take on this photographer? If you haven't, please don't. I'm working on—"

"It's too late for you to try to insinuate yourself into this," Trey interjected. "You've done enough damage."

E.D. barely held back an expletive. Insinuate? Dani had acted with lightning speed on this modeling opportunity and had ignored their one conversation where E.D. had voiced her reservations and refusal to commit without more information and a meeting with the photographer.

"Just give me the Web site address," she pleaded.

"I don't know it offhand. Do you think I have the stomach to look at it?"

"Take an antacid because the longer you allow it to stay up, the more perverts and testosterone-flooded schoolboys will be drooling over our daughter."

"I didn't say—it's being looked into," he amended sullenly.

"By whom? Damn it, give me names. That's what my office is for!"

Instead Trey hung up on her.

Breathless, impotent with fury, E.D. stared at the dead phone. Last night when he'd declared their marriage was over and that she was to blame for Dani's troubles, she'd been too dumbstruck and horrified for her daughter to really take in what was about to happen. Today with the restraining order and the appearance of her luggage, he'd humiliated her. She'd stood by and taken it, mostly because she had a case to finish, but nonetheless, she'd done nothing thinking it was all a bad dream that could somehow be worked through for the sake of the kids. But this…this set her free.

Dylan was right in his thinking. First thing in the morning, she was cutting her husband loose and going on the offensive on behalf of her daughter…and for herself.

Trey better find the common sense he hadn't shown yet and get out of her way.

Chapter Four

"You're kind to fit me into your schedule." E.D. smiled at Ivan Priestly as he beckoned her across the patio of his home toward an umbrella-covered table. It was only hours after she'd called him on this Thursday morning, and she still couldn't believe that he had not only agreed to meet with her, he'd invited her to lunch. Easing down onto the white wrought-iron chair he drew out for her, she wondered if this, too, was somehow Dylan's doing? She hoped not. Gratitude aside, her wounded self-esteem needed to believe her reputation as well as the summary over the phone had convinced this icon in their legion of her worthiness.

Smaller built and frailer than she'd expected, the famous litigator suavely took his time taking his seat to her left, which shrewdly kept his back to the sun. She noticed the hearing aid in his right ear and wondered if it was fine-tuned to capture soft sighs or to make her grit her teeth if he asked, "Pardon?" once too often because he wanted to get rid of her. She quickly got her answer.

"I have no schedule, my dear. I'm at an age where I take leisure seriously, and no longer need to suffer fools or be nice to boors because it's politically correct. I had no plans for today except to finally drag out *War and Peace* and read it in a week as has been recommended."

E.D. nodded at the tanned grandfather with his shock of white hair that looked as if it hadn't seen a comb since the last blue northern. "I have heard about your sense of principle, but I've never read as much as a whisper that you're indifferent about anything."

His laughter held private merriment. "Stay tuned. My detractors will have plenty to say when my ashes are thrown to the wind. In the meantime, you're right, the cunning remain like hyenas in the shadows and call their conduct circumspect." He gestured to the glass-topped table laden with beautiful china, fruit, a seafood salad and crackers. "Will you pour the tea? I miss my wife spoiling me and I'm sorry to say a neurological condition makes me too unsteady to do it without embarrassing us both."

She had noted his subtle trembling and immediately reached for the elegant teapot trimmed in what had to be eighteen-karat gold. "Should I leave extra room for milk?"

"No, I drink mine as is, thanks."

"Ah, a purist."

"More like a doctor's senior nurse nipping at me

like a rabid terrier to cut calories and cholesterol." Sighing, Ivan sat back in his chair and studied her. "I won't pretend any longer—I'm intrigued with your dilemma."

E.D. glanced into his wise, gray eyes and thought she saw sympathy as much as curiosity, even for a privileged child of a successful prosecutor. "I know my daughter's situation suggests an outrageous negligence."

"Which on first and second glance appears so incredibly unlike you, that I didn't easily accept it as a possibility. If anything, I see you carrying over your meticulous work patterns to where you should be a borderline suffocating mom."

She accepted his deduction with a nod that felt like an apology. "I may have ended up so, except for a life decision or two along my way." Such as whom she had chosen to marry and the demands of her job that made family often come second, whether she liked it or not. Perhaps marrying Trey had been something of a rebellion, but it had also been liberating. If so, though, she was paying—would be paying—a hefty price.

"Indeed. Which is why I suspected immediately that you're not part of this situation at all—unless you're the most foolish person ever to pass the bar, let alone become Emmett Garner's pride and joy. Since neither seems likely, it suggests a third intention more distasteful."

Momentarily lost in her thoughts, E.D. struggled. "Excuse me?"

"I'm wondering if you've been set up to carry someone else's guilt."

Hours after the first blow, she'd begun to wonder

much the same, but she hadn't yet managed to convince herself as to the why.

"Yes," he murmured studying her, "and the who is key. Stick to a narrow field."

"If my husband signed something using my name and is trying to hide it, my daughter would tell me." She would, wouldn't she? E.D. thought with less confidence than before. Naturally, Dani had her own moments of rebellion, but there'd been nothing so negative between them to warrant any behavior like this.

"I'm not saying this is representative of your situation, but my granddaughter recently got caught in such a serious fib on behalf of a friend to where she's now going to miss out on a class trip she'd greatly looked forward to and that has considerable educational impact."

As his words registered, E.D. focused only on the message behind it. "You're not going to make me go through more of an emotional wringer. You're going to take my case."

Ivan smiled as he lifted his teacup. "I hope you get some rest before your next case, Counselor."

"That's unlikely, but I'll do my best." E.D. could barely contain herself to speak the rest of her mind. "Dare I ask what else you are thinking?"

"I'm wondering why your husband was so quick to accept your guilt?"

E.D.'s pride had to take another blow. "Our marriage has expired from neglect. It's embarrassing to admit, but a fact I can't deny."

"Was that decision one-sided?"

"No, we were equally responsible." Worse than that confession, she was realizing she no longer cared, either.

"I'm simply wondering if it's feasible that he would enjoy seeing you suffering some public ridicule?" he continued.

He already had. Hopefully, it was enough. "Whatever impulses he experiences, he's not stupid. He has no income and needs my support. Ruin my career and he risks losing that comfort zone."

Ivan looked momentarily uncomfortable. "He suffers from a handicap of some sort?"

"You mean because he doesn't keep a day job himself? Only a lack of talent—he's an unsuccessful writer." As soon as the words were out, E.D. grimaced. "I'm sorry. It's too soon for me not to swan dive into bitterness."

"Understandable. How long has he been pursuing this goal of his?"

"For virtually all of our married life."

Ivan Priestly coughed behind his linen napkin. "It strikes me that you've been extremely tolerant, Ms. Martel. Who's your divorce attorney?"

"I have a dinner meeting tonight with Alyx Carmel." Noting his startled reaction, E.D. pressed, "You don't approve?"

"On the contrary, I've never met her. But from what I've seen and heard…her approach seems to go against your grain."

"Well, from where I'm sitting, my grain doesn't seem to have been serving me very well, has it?"

* * *

As she left the Priestly residence, E.D. remained lost in a maze of wonder and inspiration. Ivan was remarkable and he'd not only boosted her ego, he'd raised her optimism and buffeted her fighting instincts. Energized as she drove down the avenue back toward her office, she did a double take at the black Navigator that was heading in the opposite direction. *Dylan?* She hit her brakes and saw him cut a sharp U-turn on the otherwise empty street. He then passed her, signaling her to follow him.

Two turns later, she found herself at a small, woodsy park that was virtually empty. Bemused, she watched as he exited his vehicle and, when she released the passenger door lock, slipped into the seat beside her.

"At the risk of appearing like a stalker," he began, "I came up with two free hours and wanted to see if you were still with Ivan."

He looked elegant and smelled even better, his navy-blue suit intensifying the deep blue of his eyes. At the same time, she was dismayed that he'd ignored her plea and had taken this risk. "What if someone followed you, or me for that matter?"

"You give me far too much credit for being newsworthy. As for you, I didn't see anyone back there, did you?"

"No." E.D. checked again, though, and then came up with another concern. "You weren't planning to come in, were you? What would Ivan have said? He's admitted he's sympathetic to my case, but I doubt he would be if you appeared. He'd likely reinvent math."

Looking wholly nonplussed, Dylan replied, "I wouldn't care…would you?"

What was he saying? How could he say that?

She had to stop jumping to conclusions. He was just being a truly lovely and caring friend. "Ivan has agreed to represent me," she said going for the safest response.

"Good man!"

"I'm so grateful—and he was wonderful. Dignified, yet concerned and compassionate." Like the man who'd first come to her aid.

"Ah, E.D., I'm so relieved for you."

"Thanks." Immeasurably glad to see him on the heels of this news, she tried and almost failed to keep emotion locked in her throat and had to look away.

Dylan tenderly brushed the back of his fingers against her jawline. "It's been a helluva couple of days for you."

Couldn't he tell it was the mere sight of *him* that was turning her to mush? That the way he was looking at her tempted her to release her seat belt and throw herself into his arms? She was a married woman being carried at white-water-rapids speed into an ugly divorce and he was a professional friend—more mentor than friend—and fast becoming the dearest personal one. No, it couldn't happen with his future in such important transition.

"Well, I'd better get a grip. Emmett wouldn't take seeing me getting emotional." While she spoke out loud, the words were a warning for her alone.

"He's not here. And you're not on the clock—or he should cut you some slack all things considered."

Even his voice was a husky caress. Heaven help her. "I need to act as though I am."

"You've been dealt back-to-back emotional and psychological blows. I'd be concerned if you did succeed in behaving like a robot…or an Oscar-caliber actress."

Drawing a deep breath, E.D. glanced back at him. "Okay, confession time. I *am* glad to see you."

"Then my impulse was well worth it. When I first spotted you, I worried you'd keep driving."

"That would have been inexcusably rude."

"I'd have understood. You know what your problem is? You don't know what it's like to be supported outside of the office."

They'd never discussed their spouses before except in a cursory reference, and she wasn't sure she was ready to. "This doesn't sound like you, Dylan."

"I apologize for the bad timing, but we play the hand we're dealt. One door closes, another opens, and all that."

"What door am I supposed to be to you?"

"Ouch." He cleared his throat. "I suppose you're seeing this in the worst possible way."

She didn't want to—that was what made this conversation critical because they shouldn't be having it. Not for some time, if ever. "I apologize if I sound suspicious or ungrateful."

"You sound gun-shy and scared—which is totally understandable." Dylan lowered his head a fraction, an old habit due to his height to hold someone's gaze whether on the bench or in a toe-to-toe conversation. "I simply want you to understand that I'm here for you, E.D."

She studied him a moment longer then turned away again to digest what she'd taken in. Hoping to slow what was beginning to feel increasingly, intensely, intimate, she added, "I can only imagine what Trey's reaction will be to Ivan's suspicions of him. Ivan thinks if Dani didn't forge my name, Trey did."

After a slight pause, Dylan asked, "Do you agree?"

"At this point, I suppose nothing should surprise me. But what happened to make either of them willing to do that? To hurt me to protect themselves?"

"You're sure this isn't a case of a terrible misunder-standing?"

"Even if it is—which I doubt—what he said and did the other night and yesterday makes excuses an impos-sibility." E.D. had to swallow the frozen block wedged in her throat. "No one prepares you for this kind of betrayal, Dylan."

This time when he reached out, he cupped his hand at her nape beneath her neat chignon. "I can't imagine."

"He should have just asked or at least challenged me. I deserved that much. He had to know I would give him the benefit of the doubt if things were reversed."

"Generous of you to credit him with your sense of logic and fair play."

E.D. felt another stab that made it all the harder to breathe. "Imagine coming to the realization at this point and position in my career that I don't know the man anymore. Maybe I never did. What does that say for me as a litigator?"

"I think you should come to the condo. It's only a few blocks from here."

Gathering herself, she shook her head enough to encourage him to remove his hand. "Impossible. I have to get back—and you have to stop being so reckless."

"Determined, not reckless," he said softly.

E.D. frowned at him. "Dylan, have you had a bad health checkup or something? You're acting—scary."

"I've never felt more clearheaded in my life."

She could barely think when he locked those dark blue eyes on hers. "Okay, dare I threaten a gentle censure for some bad timing?"

"You want to hear about timing, Eva Danielle?" Dylan worked her right hand free from the steering wheel to transfer it into his warm grasp. "I've been dealing with the results of that for almost twenty years." He glanced down at her modestly manicured fingernails painted only with clear polish. "I should have followed a gut hunch the moment you extended this hand the night we met."

Torn between pulling free and tightening her fingers, E.D. all but choked. "Sure. I always have that effect on people. When I got home that night, I found four voice messages from the president, governor and two senators."

"You didn't sense I was captivated by you from the moment you welcomed me with that smile?"

"Frankly, no. And my mouth was so dry, it's a miracle I could speak, while you were kind and patient with everyone who gushed over you."

Dylan tightened his grasp. "E.D., I was one step away from suggesting we ditch the seminar that night and find a cozy pub booth."

She wouldn't, couldn't, believe it. Oh, she knew

he'd admired a smiling blonde but he never could have taken it beyond that. "You had too much professional integrity. Besides, you were engaged to Brenda."

"And you were seriously dating Trey."

It was disturbing how easily her husband slipped from her mind when in Dylan's presence. "Brenda was right for you. She understood how hard you had to work, and had the generosity and willingness to support that."

"I won't disagree. She was a lovely person and a good partner."

"I don't want to think how my husband is going to describe me in hindsight. I suppose all I can hope for is to never be near him again when holding a sharp object." She'd aimed for humor—somewhat—and came up unconvincing.

"How *do* you think Trey conceives your marriage?"

"I—" *Honestly hadn't thought of that in years.* E.D. looked at her hand in Dylan's and gently disengaged herself. "I can't have this conversation. Not with you, not now."

"We can't always get the timing we want, and history has proved we both made decisions based on mitigating circumstances."

"But I have two children, Dylan, and I need to be focused on them."

"Agreed. That said, when I turned on the TV yesterday, heard your name, and saw the wolves licking their chops and circling in, I felt things I don't even have words for yet."

She risked a great deal to meet his steady gaze and

felt it in places long shut down and repressed. "You got me through yesterday. I was fantasizing about sending a personal note once you were confirmed and then burying myself deep in work again. Maybe you should have waited. Maybe you should have let that call be enough."

"That's one option. The other is that if you're going to take one step, you might as well take two." Dylan bent to place a kiss on the back of her hand. "I'll stop. Just make me one promise—don't lock me out?"

Chapter Five

E.D. didn't lock out Dylan, but fate intervened elsewhere and business forced Alyx Carmel to postpone her meeting with E.D. until Friday evening. It was just as well because E.D. already felt run through the wringer by the end of Thursday, and Dylan's declaration certainly compounded that.

Alyx ultimately invited E.D. for dinner to her home in a posh Austin neighborhood. E.D. brought a bottle of pinot noir that a trusted wine expert in her office had recommended. Because of Alyx's reputation as a true professional, she was surprised by the invitation to meet away from an office environment. Alyx was notoriously private and no one seemed to know anything about her personal life except that she was single and rejected all personal social invitations. Naturally, that triggered some comments about her sexuality. E.D. didn't care one iota about that; she had enough of her own concerns to deal with. Then, upon pulling into Alyx's driveway, she was met by a uniformed cop who stepped from his squad car parked out front. That triggered different concerns.

While the officer didn't smile, he also didn't rest his hand on his holstered gun in a way to suggest he thought her a threat. Small gifts, E.D. thought, wondering what was up now.

"ID, ma'am."

This wasn't a gated community and Alyx hadn't warned her of trouble. Wondering if she was about to get back into the evening news again, she reached for her purse. "I'm E. D. Martel… D.A.'s office," she added because although she'd met many of Austin's finest in court, she hadn't yet met this gentleman and wanted to send a signal that they were on the same team. "I have a dinner appointment with Ms. Carmel."

Although he nodded as though he already knew that, he went through the motions of inspecting her driver's license, then handed it back. "Thank you. Please be sure to lock your vehicle as you proceed inside."

"Is there something wrong, Officer—?"

"Just a precaution, ma'am. Have a pleasant night."

Alyx was already at the door as E.D. made her way up the walkway; an apology was clearly visible in her face.

"Forgive me," the brunette said upon holding the wrought-iron-and-glass door wide. "A situation has developed and I thought it would be easier for both of us if we met here." Closing and locking the storm door, she then did the same with the ornately carved interior one, testing each action. "A client's ex has escaped from jail and I was advised it would be wise to ask for some protection until he's back in custody."

E.D. wasn't entirely okay about learning this without being given a chance to reschedule, despite the capable-looking officer outside. On the other hand, she knew firsthand how you couldn't always control such things. "Does it appear that's going to happen soon?"

Alyx tightened her full lips before replying. "Not as fast as any of us would like, and because he promised to butcher my client and leave me alive just long enough to explain what he thought of both of us, I couldn't refuse the chief's offer for extra protection. I'd understand completely if you chose not to stay…or opted to seek other counsel."

E.D. was tempted, but knew Alyx was the tops in her specialty, which was why she'd sought her out in the first place. Resigned to wade through this the hard way, E.D. nodded and set her bag and briefcase on the vibrant red armchair with an exquisite ivory cashmere throw draped over the back. "If you trust the officer outside is capable, then I do, too. I'm sorry you're having to go through this." She held out her hand. "Good to see you again."

Alyx was a tall, curvaceous woman, a throwback to the pin-up models of the forties and fifties, complete with lush chestnut waves resting on her shoulders and smoky, come hither gray eyes. It was said that more soon-to-be ex-husbands tripped up during depositions from staring too long at her than criminals did during good cop–bad cop interrogations. But tonight her allure was muted: the skillfully applied makeup about worn off, her hair more hand mussed than artful, and she was wearing jeans and a thin black tunic top instead of the usual figure-enhancing business suit. She looked, E.D. concluded, ready to leap out of a window if necessary, and run as though the devil were grabbing for her shadow.

Grasping her hand briefly, but firmly, Alyx continued, "Thanks. You, too. But frankly, I'd love to have the opportunity for a face-to-face with this piece of scum." She nodded to the compact .38 on the coffee table next to a glass of red wine. "This is one of those situations when you're tempted to save the taxpayer, not to mention this jerk's long-suffering wife and kids, court costs, as well as the price of years of incarceration."

E.D. nodded in understanding; she'd been encouraged to keep a gun herself, but never had, concerned that with the children around, something could be forgotten and things end up worse off. "Has this happened often?" TV seemed to be full of such incidents these days.

"I'm not going to lie to you, E.D.," Alyx said on a sigh. "I've gone to two clients' funerals since beginning my practice. I only pray this situation won't require a third." She gestured to the two ivory leather couches facing each other. "Have a seat, can I get you a glass of wine? Something else to drink? Or would you like to start your salad now?"

"I really don't think I should indulge considering that I haven't eaten more than a bite in the last two days." E.D. had forced herself to nibble on the crepes

Ivan's housekeeper had served, but otherwise nothing. "I hope you didn't go to too much trouble." She handed over the bottle. "Maybe this will come in handy for a celebration later?"

"Thank you. Oh—" Alyx brightened at inspecting the gift "—lovely. Let me pour you a small glass. It's the same as what I'm drinking. Really, E.D., you couldn't have been kinder, and I know this will bolster you."

There was nothing to say without insulting her hostess, so E.D. smiled politely and when Alyx returned and handed her the small glass, she wet her lips with the mellow wine while Alyx assumed a seat on the opposite couch. "It's good. Being no connoisseur, I'm delighted you approve." Wanting badly to get to business, she added, "Were you surprised that I phoned you?"

Alyx flicked her fingers, the nails painted a tantalizing nude. "Nothing surprises me anymore. What did have me wondering was why you married Trey in the first place. Pardon my bluntness, but he's always seemed such a low achiever. So to answer your question, I suppose I should confess to being somewhat proud that you called. I hate to be disappointed in my opinions of people."

"I have no apology let alone a defense for my marriage other than my children," E.D. said, brushing the lipstick off the edge of her glass with her thumb. "I will say you are a startling but refreshing change of pace— even for this veteran prosecutor."

"You said Ivan Priestly is handling your suit against

the photographer? Excellent. Then we'll refer to Sleazeball One as the soon-to-be *ex*-photographer."

"I hope you're right. Otherwise, the stay-at-home-mom idea is sounding increasingly the smarter route to have taken."

"Don't get me wrong. I've seen it go both ways. But tell me this…how has Trey acted toward you up until this mushroomed?"

"We've been polite strangers for—" E.D. tried and couldn't remember "—well, it's been coming on for some time."

"Do you sleep in the same bed?"

Embarrassment mounting, E.D. took another breath. "We have a king-size one and we're rarely in it at the same time."

"Your love life sounds as rotten as mine."

E.D. decided to take a leap of faith. "On an occasion or two he accused me of emasculating him."

"Did you have a knife in your hand at the time?"

"Maybe I was tempted, but no."

"Sorry, couldn't resist the joke." Alyx tilted her head. "I know you're a tough prosecutor, but I suspect you shed that persona too easily for your family… and he's full of you-know-what. At the risk of upsetting you further, I've got to give you this piece of advice. Do yourself a favor and if you have slept with him—in the biblical sense—in the last year, get a blood test."

Startled, E.D. blinked. "Excuse me?"

"Trey's what? Forty-something? If that man has managed to keep his hands off of you, either he's impotent, or he's messing around one way or another. Protect yourself. Get tested."

E.D. thought of her reclusive, quiet husband with his dimpled smile, slight paunch and thinning hair. While he wasn't seriously overweight, he wasn't into exercise and he had less muscle tone than a newborn. Trey cheating? She took another sip of her wine to keep from laughing—probably hysterically. "I think that's the one thing I don't have to worry about."

"Reconsider." Alyx leaned forward in her seat. "There's nothing integral or intimate left between you and yet suddenly without giving you any warning he demands a divorce? This situation with the photographs is an excuse. He's having an *affair*."

"Excuse me, if I call to check on the kids or a repair, he's there to answer, or else he picks me up on the cell because he's at the market or something like that." As much as E.D. doubted the possibility, it might almost be interesting to think of Trey trying something on the side.

"Then let's have him followed. I contract a guy who's reliable. I'll bet you a lunch that his photos show more than your oh-so-righteous spouse squeezing canta-loupes, and wipe your daughter's problems off the map."

"You sound…I don't know, more hurt than angry."

It had been just past eleven o'clock when E.D. had returned to Dylan's ranch, but once she'd changed into her Japanese silk pjs, she'd done what the message on his answering machine had asked and returned his call. As she lay on the bed and stared up at the beamed ceiling, she sighed. "Not so much hurt as offended, which is foolish because there's probably nothing to her theory."

"You said yourself that Alyx Carmel is a pretty good judge of character."

"Fine, but I've lived with him for seventeen years."

"Maybe making you too close to the situation to see what's in front of you," Dylan said carefully. "Or what if you're not ready to face that you might have wanted this to happen?"

E.D. caught her breath. Could that be true? Had she been pushing Trey away into the arms of another woman so that she could be free herself, without having to deal with any guilt? That Dylan should be the messenger of this idea gave her pause.

As though reading her mind, Dylan muttered, "Forget I said that."

Too late. E.D.'s mind raced...Brenda had died eleven months ago. While she and Trey hadn't made love for a month or better before that, was it possible that she'd consciously or unconsciously increased the distance between them after the funeral?

"E.D., talk to me. I didn't mean to insinuate—"

"No, you've both forced me to look at myself, at my motives. I may not be liking it much, but I sense the need."

"Hey, if he is having an affair, he made the decision instead of fighting for his marriage. What's more, he's using Dani's misfortune as a means to hide his deceit. That makes him a lot of things, none of which is a victim."

"I know, but I'm half the reason there's nothing left to fight for. What does that make me?"

"A hardworking woman who for too long wasn't being appreciated or loved."

"I don't deserve being put on a pedestal, Dylan, and I'm no Joan of Arc."

"I'm relieved to hear the latter because you've sacrificed enough for the lazy bum as it is." A smile crept into his voice. "So Alyx is going on the offensive. Good for her."

E.D. thought of how troubled her ex-classmate had looked. "I feel badly for her. She's under twenty-four-hour protection."

"What?"

She filled him in on Alyx's dilemma.

Dylan swore softly. "Tell me you were ultra careful as you drove home?"

Turning onto her side, she gazed at the pillow beside her and felt a warm glow at the word *home*. "Of course. If I'd suspected anything, I would have called 9-1-1 and driven straight for the police station."

"Considering the climate for violence these days," he said, sounding anything but reassured, "I think it should be a given that there's daily escorting for judges by the police, at least to and from their residences."

"You'll deserve that especially."

"I was thinking about you. The people who come to my court, or the next should I get the seat, have been behind bars for a long time. We aren't in imminent danger."

"Tell that to the judge in Georgia who was killed in his own courtroom. But—to end this on a lovelier note— it was wonderful to see you today," she added softly.

"Want to see me again?"

"Yes," was on the tip of her tongue, but the left side of her brain triggered some mute button and filled her mind with why she shouldn't reply and think instead of "must dos."

"Wrong answer."

E.D. all but moaned. "It's not fair to tempt me."

"It's all I'm allowed to do in this environment."

"I have a new case starting Monday. One briefcase alone is full of material I need to read. Another is the work I should have done instead of my meetings with Ivan and Alyx. And even so, I hope to sneak by the civic center and catch Mac at his weekly chess meet."

"Won't Trey be there?"

"He's not a big fan of the game. If I couldn't take him, Mac would catch a ride with a friend. I'm hoping that's still the case."

"Trey is sounding increasingly dull to me," Dylan drawled. "What about later?"

How he tempted her. "It's impossible. There's just too much at stake."

"I need to see you."

The word *need* spawned an aching deep in her womb. Nevertheless it was a word with a meaning vastly different than *should* or *must*.

"Don't you want to see me again?"

"I'm going to hang up now," E.D. replied. "Good night and thank you so much."

"You're a hard woman."

No, but her nipples were. Touching one as it thrust against the silky satin, she repressed a shiver. "You've already made it impossible for me to concentrate on work, don't make it impossible for me to sleep."

"Are you in bed?"

"Yes."

He made a low sound. "What are you wearing?"

She chuckled softly. "Satin. Black."

This time he sighed. "I wish I could see you."

"I'm going to hang up now before this becomes painful."

"Hell, it already is. Sweet dreams, Eva Danielle."

"You, too," she whispered, and gently replaced the receiver onto the cradle. Then she rolled over onto her stomach and moaned into the pillow.

Chapter Six

Like an ant colony abuzz with activity, chess players at the civic center scurried about to find an opponent. Many of the younger players had one or both of their parents tagging after them, and E.D. barely avoided getting run over by a woman charging down an aisle with a double stroller. E.D. was preoccupied herself trying to spot her eleven-year-old son, Mackenzie, and at the same time avoid Trey if he was here.

When a burly man with shoulders as wide as the game tables stepped aside, her gaze immediately fell on the skinny, bespectacled youth sitting at the farthest table near the corner of the room. Her heart wrenched with love and compassion. Mac sat alone staring at the board, his rumpled blue polo shirt turned inside out and his hair looking as if he'd suffered a restless night.

E.D. knew immediately that he was dreading the chance of being the last chosen—or if an odd number of players showed, ending up with no player at all. The urge to rescue him had her forcing herself backward; she knew he'd never forgive her if she treated him like a child in front of so many people.

To her surprise and relief, only seconds later she saw a young man at least twice his age step up to the table, speak, and extend his hand. When Mac shook it, the college-age man took a seat and the two immediately fell into serious play.

Glancing around to look for the best place to watch and still stay out of sight, E.D.'s gaze suddenly locked with Trey's. Although he didn't look much more awake than Mac, the anger in his gray eyes had her spinning around and rushing for the exit. She didn't want to appear intimidated by him, but she would rather give that impression than be involved in a scene that would draw in her son.

Barely into the main hall, she felt the determined grip of his fingers closing around her upper arm. Then the rude jerk swung her backward and around to face him.

"You were warned to keep your distance. I can yell for security to haul you in for this."

Looking from his hand's cruel grasp to her husband, E.D. firmly wrenched free, wishing she could tell him exactly what he could do with that restraining order. Unfortunately, she couldn't afford a trip to the police station that, one way or another, would be picked up by the press.

"You have never misjudged me more than in this

matter, Trey," she said with quiet conviction. "I realize that you would love for me to create a scene to actually give you something to accuse me of, but you know what? I'm not the idiot you take me for. A fool, yes, for believing in you several years too many, for trusting you by your word, and for respecting you as a man of principle."

Aware that a few people had grown curious and slowed to observe and eavesdrop, E.D. spun on her heel and left. At least she'd had a chance to see her son, she thought. She would hang on to that small positive.

As she walked toward the parking lot, she heard her name called out. Spinning around, she saw gangly Mac running toward her. One look at his anxious face and slipping glasses, she retraced several steps and spread her arms to catch him against her.

"Sweetheart, please be careful. You can't risk an asthma attack."

"Why are you leaving?"

"I have to, Mac. Legally, I can't be near you right now without your father's permission."

"This is crazy," he gasped between pants. "I'll tell him that I want you here."

"Where's your inhaler?" E.D. replied with a pointed look to his jeans' pocket. As he drew it out and pumped, she finger-combed his hair. "I don't want him upset with you, too. It's enough that I got to see you for a second. That looks like a tough opponent in there, you'd better get back to your game."

"He's the captain of the UT chess team. He's waiting for me and told me to take a minute to talk to you.

He cut his teeth on this group and says I could do real competition."

"Oh, wow." While secretly pleased, E.D. made a mental note to check into the young man to see if he was all he claimed to be. Good grief, she thought, if she couldn't trust her husband, why trust a stranger being kind to her gentle, shy son? But she hugged Mac again. "That's quite a compliment. Can't say I'm too surprised, though."

Mac's slender face grew flushed. "Thanks, Mom. You would be good, too, if you practiced more. I miss our games."

"Me, too."

His sweet face—no longer childlike, but years away from adult strength and definition—grew pensive. "What's gonna happen?"

"I'm only slightly more informed than you are, so all I can assure you of is that we'll get through this. Try to be patient."

"If you guys are divorcing, I should get visitation rights."

Feeling claws in the fingers that clutched her heart, E.D. swallowed at the latest tightness in her throat. "That'll happen, I promise. Please just focus on your health—and your schoolwork."

"Don't worry, I am. It's the only way to ignore Dani. If she's not screaming at Dad, she's slamming doors and crying in her room. She refused to go to school yesterday."

It wasn't the first time Dani had played the diva; she was an intense, theatrical and strong-minded girl who was struggling to find anything beneficial in those characteristics, while juggling the negatives that came with being a teenager. But if her daughter was fighting with Trey—whom she usually wrapped around her little finger—things were at critical mass.

"I'm so sorry things are in upheaval," E.D. said rubbing Mac's back before putting him at arm's length. No need for her perceptive child to feel her heart racing like a scared-witless racehorse. "It won't last. I promise."

"Good, 'cuz Dad's acting pretty edgy himself. And forgetful."

"About what?"

"Appointments, laundry not done, no milk in the house."

Interesting. Of course, she had always made the lists in the family; Trey had simply followed directives. So many assumed he did it all solo—she learned at neighborhood block parties or at functions after church—but that wasn't true. E.D.'s detoxing time was about keeping her fingers in the domestic nuts and bolts of home.

"How about you do me a favor and handle the grocery list for a few days?" she asked him. "You're the most organized one in the family."

He grinned. "Next to you. Cool. Okay. The first thing I'll do is keep cilantro off the list. Ever since Dani's dance teacher shared a recipe, Dad's been killing us with the stuff."

Over his head, E.D. saw that Trey had lost his patience and was about to come after them. "Your father wants you back inside. Love you, Mac. I know he's told you not to call, but if you need me, you have my cell number, right?"

"He's taken your number out of my phone, but I have it memorized."

Silently cursing her estranged spouse, E.D. swallowed and managed a quick kiss on her son's forehead. "Talk to you soon. Now go."

With a last hug, the boy started back to the building.

"Hey," E.D. called after him. When he glanced back, she plucked at the shell under her blazer.

Mac glanced down at his shirt and gave a brief "Ha!" With a parting wave, he resumed his retreat while yanking the shirt over his head, turning it right side out, then slipping it on again.

Shaking her head because the result was that his hair looked more disheveled than before, E.D. managed a wry smile and proceeded to her car. She hoped hearing her son's brief merriment would sustain her the rest of the day.

When Dylan entered his ranch by mid-afternoon, he wasn't surprised to be met by Chris midway down the meandering driveway.

"How goes it?" he asked as his caretaker and foreman dismounted his horse and came to shake his hand.

"Quiet. Ms. Martel is at the house. She went out just before eight this morning and returned less than two hours later. Been inside ever since."

No doubt burying herself in work to avoid worrying about her kids, Dylan thought. "Any other traffic at the gate?"

"Nope. Should I expect anyone? Trouble?"

Dylan glanced over his shoulder, considering how

much to say. He trusted Chris as much as anyone, otherwise the cowboy wouldn't have the job he held; Dylan simply didn't see the point in starting trouble when it might not be necessary. "Probably not, but there's an escaped convict headlined in the news."

"I heard something about that on the news. Didn't note anything tying it to Ms. Martel."

"I don't think she's ever met him, but since the targeted attorney has dealings with her, it wouldn't hurt to keep in mind that he's a rapist and murderer and to be considered armed and dangerous."

Chris touched the brim of his hat. "I hear you."

After they discussed the lack of rain, pasture conditions and Chris updated him on the condition of their modest herd, Dylan continued on to the house. Things did appear quiet. When here himself, the doors remained unlocked, but considering why E.D. was here, not to mention the baggage Alyx brought to the situation, he was glad to find it locked and was cautious as he slid his key into the dead bolt and entered the house.

Just inside the foyer, he saw E.D. asleep on one of the couches. Two stacks of files were piled on the carved coffee table and an assortment of affidavits and depositions lay scattered around her on the couch and hardwood floor. With her blond hair spilling over handwoven cushions, and her lacy chemise providing a tempting view of her willowy shape and flawless skin, Dylan could only stand there for a moment and drink in the vision she made.

As though feeling his gaze, her lashes fluttered. When she opened her eyes, she stared as though not sure he was real. "Dylan."

"I'm sorry for waking you. I know you're exhausted."

She looked a little self-conscious and disorientated as she sat up. When the pad, pen and papers on her lap started sliding off, she muttered and grappled to catch what she could.

"No, no, it's—blast—I was just having a power nap."

She shoved everything onto the cushion beside her and stood. Her next glance spoke of uncertainty and embarrassment. Dylan understood why. He'd never seen her dressed in anything less than professional or formal attire, her hair perfectly coifed. Now, her blond waves tumbled to her collarbone in sexy dishabille; her chemise was a cotton-lace confection, the first two buttons undone and exposing more of her feminine allure. With her jeans delineating coltish long legs, she pretty much resembled the coed who had mesmerized him years ago.

"It's just past three," he told her watching as she checked her watch, fingered the first button of her top and abruptly, self-consciously, crossed her arms. "I knew you'd work hard and wouldn't eat."

"I guess I forgot."

Dylan nodded to the bag cradled in his left arm. "Since I needed to stop by and see Chris anyway, I thought I'd pick up something for dinner. It's just the basics: steak, baking potatoes and vegetables for a salad."

After eyeing the bag only a second, her gaze fell to her near-empty iced-tea glass. "I need a refill."

Dylan frowned as she picked it up, only to be momentarily sidetracked by a brief glimpse of cleavage and the lacy edge of her bra. His mouth dry, he followed her to the kitchen.

Barefoot, E.D. was now several inches shorter than he was. As much as he admired the elegant attorney, the casual one made him ache with a new level of longing, even down to her feet, which were unadorned except for clear nail polish. Not so much as one toe ring. His own secretary, Paulie, owned one, an affectionate challenge from a granddaughter that she kept in her top desk drawer and threatened to wear if she ever became stylish enough to come to work without panty hose. The amusing thought didn't provide him with any clues as to how to respond to E.D.'s unusual mood; therefore, he opted for frankness.

"You're upset with me," he said.

"This is your home, Dylan. If I'd been thinking clearly, I'd have considered there are things you need to do here, so why shouldn't you have access to your kitchen instead of waiting for dinner until you were back in town?"

What kind of answer was that? "I wanted to do something for you. Spend a little time with you."

Setting the sack on the center counter, he watched her place her glass nearby and head for the refrigerator. "But we discussed that and agreed it wasn't wise."

"True. On the other hand, like you, I was observant about being followed."

"Thank you. That isn't the point, though."

Apparently not. Determined to find out what was, he continued, "I also concluded—undoubtedly correctly—that you wouldn't feed yourself properly."

Not only didn't she respond to that, she was avoiding meeting his eyes.

As she reached for the refrigerator, Dylan decided he would be damned if he was going to let her keep walking on eggshells around him and treating him like some eastern untouchable. They'd lost enough time as it was. Years.

In two steps, he cut her off and framed her face with his hands. He felt her instinctive stiffening, heard the soft catch of her breath, and her brown eyes—usually wise and analytic—went wide with dismay. "Okay, I was a bad boy," he said gruffly. "But after last night's conversation, how do you expect me to stay away? Let me answer that."

Before she could respond, he lowered his head. The first brush of his lips against hers sent an electric current through him just as he expected it would. His entire body tense with restraint, he slanted his mouth across hers and imbibed—the silken smoothness of her lips, her soft moan and her warm breath. A deeper hunger stirred him from his long, forced coma, prompting him to seek more, drink in her essence, then her subtle sigh as he stroked his tongue against hers. He let his fingers seek and explore the incredible wealth of her hair, while he drew deep the mysterious, yet mystical scent of lily of the valley. It flirted and tempted his senses like an evasive memory.

Dylan wanted and needed to have her closer; it had been ages since he'd held a woman against him; longer since he'd craved that experience. But he wasn't about to press his luck.

Raising his head, he gazed into her bright eyes. "At least that's out of the way."

"Oh, Dylan, this is such a mistake."

"The tension was starting to hurt everything else, second only to the curiosity to see what it would be like between us."

"So we move on to the 'what could it hurt' temptation?"

At least she didn't call it *phase*, he thought dryly. With each word, her warm breath caressed him, and while she didn't push him to arm's distance, her gaze grew increasingly brooding. "Eva Danielle," he murmured, "temptation is a given around you."

"Don't." This time she did ease herself from his grasp. "This is what you call help?"

As she stepped to the counter and gripped the edge, Dylan reached out to stroke her back, only to drop his hand. "Sorry. The more I think about it, the more I believe I'd be of greater comfort if I could hold you when you're troubled, kiss you when you're tired and hurting." He wanted to now.

E.D. studied him solemnly. "I've never been kissed the way you just kissed me. I've been so wanting you to."

The pressure in his chest grew painful. Happiness wasn't supposed to hurt. "I'd feel better if you said that without it sounding like there was a *but* coming."

"There has to be. I have no right to this, Dylan."

Now *that* scared the hell out of him, so much so that he kept silent and waited for the rest in fear of making a nuclear bomb–size error. All the certificates and credentials in his office were useless in figuring out how to navigate this.

"Yes, my marriage is over," E.D. continued, "but I'm not about to do something to endanger my chances for suing for custody of my kids."

Dylan inclined his head. "Understood."

"At the same time, you have no right—after working so hard, after others have supported your rise to the next level—to throw away a career with such incredible potential."

"That doesn't mean we can't—"

She shifted to touch her index finger to his lips. "I see how this is lining up and you *are* going to get this seat on the bench, and another, all of which will demand sacrifices. I can't add to that burden. You don't deserve being linked to my baggage."

She was adorable and obstinate. Dylan worked for a comic grimace. "When do I get a vote?"

"You don't. You *are* the romantic, the white knight. You act as though because your intentions are good and your nose is clean that everything will work out happily ever after."

"Aw, c'mon. You know better than that." Despite the lazy response, he continued to study her and with that came a growing hunch that her skittishness was due to a recent incident. "Something else happened today. Did it make matters worse?"

E.D. took a defensive stance on the other side of the counter. "Not worse, just the usual piling on," she said rubbing her forehead. "I went to Mac's chess meet this morning."

"I don't know how risky that was, but I hope he wanted to talk to you?"

"Oh, he did…except that Trey was there. And before and after, so did Trey."

That was enough for Dylan to draw conclusions. "He wouldn't let you have a few moments with your son?"

"Barely, once Mac ran after me." Crossing her arms again, E.D. shrugged. "Poor Mac is so confused and stressed, he's using up his inhaler in record time. I just hope he remembered to tell Trey that he needed to stop by the pharmacy."

Knowing better than to go to her as he longed to do, Dylan pretended a casualness he might never feel again and began unpacking the groceries. The first item was a bottle of Shiraz. He figured they could both use a glass at this stage. By the time he got the stemware and corkscrew, he noticed that E.D. had buttoned her camisole. Foregoing the temptation to ask her if she thought that made her any less desirable to him, he ripped off the plastic seal from the bottle.

"Did Trey threaten you?"

"Trey is feeling his power. Who's boosting his batteries, I've yet to determine."

"Or oats."

At Dylan's dark look, E.D. shrugged. "It's already been suggested, and I'm sorry, but that's laughable. We're talking his usual passive-aggressive behavior, nothing else."

Dylan's grip on the neck of the bottle tightened. "Excuse me? With a comment like that I'd have recommended leaving the slug long ago. Passive-aggressive from the man you support and have borne children to?" He swore silently. "Speaking as a man who had yearned for children, I seriously resent that."

E.D.'s answering glance held pure chagrin. "And have probably lost all respect for me. One thing, though, I did make sure he never said anything disrespectful to me or about our relationship in front of the kids. At the worst they think we're like polite strangers."

"No wonder he's managing to keep them from calling you. They don't have a clue as to what a worm he really is—or what you've done for him *and* them."

"Can we change the subject, please?"

Once he had the cork out, Dylan poured the wine and handed her the glass. "I'm sorry for vocalizing too much. I'm just upset for you." He touched his glass to hers. "Here's to more appealing subjects. Know of any?"

With a reluctant smile, E.D. touched her glass to his and took a sip of the wine. Instantly, her expression changed to appreciation. "Oh, that's divine. I'd better start on the salad or this will go to my head fast."

As she washed her hands, Dylan finished unpacking the grocery sack; folding it, he stored it where he kept the reusable sacks. Then he went outside to light the gas grill.

"I'm glad you like variety greens as a salad," E.D. said upon his return. She was draining the rinsed leaves in the colander. "What else?"

He pointed to the pantry. "Pecans? How do you feel about them?"

"Along with the feta you brought?" She leaned over to peer at the small container. "Is it goat or sheep's milk? Ah, goat. I try to have it often when lunching out. Trey loathes it."

Why was he not surprised? "I know yellow onions contain more antitoxins, but the purple I chose taste the best with that mix. Unless you want to leave them out entirely...? Your call."

"Are you kidding? A half recipe isn't a recipe."

Dylan chuckled. "You've got that right."

"Does that mean you mix your own oil-and-vinegar dressing?"

"Adding a touch of white wine—there should be some in the fridge—balsamic vinegar, and olive oil over on the far counter."

For the most part, they worked harmoniously together; there were moments of bumped elbows or self-consciousness, brief touches that seemed more intentional than accidental that happened between people who weren't yet intimate, but wanted to be. Conversation was sporadic, yet Dylan found reassurance believing that E.D. was okay in those stretches of silence.

"What's that?"

Her question tugged him out of his introspection. "Just salt." He'd scrubbed the potatoes and had forked them a bit. Now he was sprinkling them before wrapping them in aluminum foil.

"It's as chunky as rock salt."

"It's kosher salt...or you can use sea salt. It's what they use for baked potatoes in restaurants. Supposed to have less something or other in it. I don't always re-member the nutritional data."

"You're doing way better than me. When I get home in time to eat dinner, I settle for what's prepared, other-wise you know the drill—grab what's left in the fridge or the peanut butter." E.D. leaned into him. "Am I seeing a hint of a long-repressed fantasy of yours? Restaura-teur?"

"Hardly. I think there's a profession that works more hours than deputy district attorneys and interns. No, it was when Brenda couldn't manage the house anymore that I began taking over things for the housekeeper on weekends, cooking being one of them."

"From the looks of this, you enjoyed it."

Dylan paused and looked out the glass doors. "You know, as sad as it was for Brenda, it was also a time of contentment for us."

"How sweet. I'm glad. I'll bet she lived for those weekends with you."

"I hope so," he replied quietly. He had tried hard to be what Brenda had needed in the end, and he had never betrayed her, except in the occasional daydream. Since then he'd been on a few dates, which were better described as dinner with sex. Not one of his compan-ions had cared a bit about his late wife or how he felt about her passing. That E.D. sincerely did made him want to haul her into his arms in simple gratitude. Problem was, this was her time over the rough road and he knew how to travel rough terrain. Finishing with the potatoes, he closed the foil and carried them out to the grill.

* * *

"This was wonderful." Glass in hand, E.D. relaxed against the back of the cushioned deck chair and sighed at the other half of her huge T-bone and potato. "I can wrap this for dinner tomorrow."

"Oh, no you don't," Dylan said, pushing his own clean plate away. "Chris has a cow dog named Lefty who'll feel pretty left out if I don't deliver these bones on my way out. I guarantee that dog has his nose in the air this minute and is sitting at attention waiting for them."

"Really? I haven't seen or heard a dog."

"He's well trained. If Chris tells him to stay put at the cabin or elsewhere, Lefty is a sentinel, and the only time you'll hear him bark is if he's herding a stubborn cow, or warning Chris about a snake or coyotes."

E.D. listened and watched Dylan with rapt attention. Wise or not, she was grateful that he'd come. He'd managed to get her mind off her troubles, and heaven knows she'd needed the break from work. "If you had to do it over again, would you have become a full-time rancher like your grandfather?" She could easily see him in a Stetson and boots.

He sipped his wine and first responded with a one-shouldered shrug. "I doubt it. Even when I was a kid, Gramps warned that it was becoming an increasingly tough business, financially speaking. And truth be known, he'd liked to brag about having a JAG officer son and was always encouraging me to follow my father into law."

Sadly, Dylan's father and mother had been killed

when Dylan was in college, during a twenty-fifth wedding-anniversary trip to Europe. His grandfather, long widowed, had passed only a year before. It struck E.D. again how she knew his background almost better than she knew Trey's.

"The stock we raise pays the taxes as well as Chris's salary," Dylan continued. "I'm grateful for that. The longer I can keep this out of the hands of developers, the happier I'll be."

"I wish you had family still living to see how far you've come." Or children. Did he miss that? He was only forty-two. It could still happen—if he met the right woman.

"Things work out the way they do. I'm too pragmatic to get mired in the could-have, would-have, should-have mindset." He cast her a sidelong look. "Well, for the most part."

E.D. felt that look and another surge of warmth spread through her that had little to do with the sun, still above the western horizon. "I for one have to admit I'm grateful my mother didn't make it to see my situation." She'd passed last year after a thankfully short illness. E.D.'s father had been a smoker and had died of lung cancer the year after E.D. had passed the bar. "She was such a strong woman and would have been supportive, but she wouldn't have hesitated noting that Trey wasn't right for me."

"You took after her in the frankness department."

"Quite a bit. When I'm dealing with an annoying defense attorney, I mimic her Grace Kelly coolness or aloofness. It usually has the individual backing off and pouting like a rejected high-schooler."

Dylan chuckled. "I want to come see you in action one of these days. I've been meaning to. I bet every male, from the defense team to the jury, has his tongue hanging out of his mouth."

The mere thought of him in the same courtroom had her setting down her glass for fear of the contents resembling a lake in an earthquake. "More like gritting their teeth wishing I'd get on my broom and stop making their lives miserable." Either the wine or his caressing gaze was getting to her, but she didn't want to talk about work even when he was flattering her. She rose to clear the patio table.

"Now what do you think you're doing?" Dylan asked, rising himself.

"I've played hooky about all that I can afford. As much as I've enjoyed this, I need to get back to those files inside."

He took her plate from her hand. "I'll clean up. You go on ahead."

"That's hardly fair."

But he insisted, and as she had enough reading material for two people, she gratefully returned to the living room and was soon lost in study. She couldn't say how much time had passed when a mug of steaming coffee appeared on the coffee table. On the edge of the oversize saucer were several butter cookies dipped in chocolate.

"To help you endure the tedious part of things. I'm off to treat Lefty." Dylan swung the baggy containing the steak bones.

Smiling, E.D. touched his hand. "Thank you…for everything."

"Thank you for not staying upset with me."

The moment had come for her to walk him to the door. However, if she did, she knew he would kiss her, probably with the same sensuality as before. How could she let him without letting down all of her guards and asking for more?

"Stay put."

The hand on her shoulder startled her. She hadn't realized she'd begun to rise. When Dylan took hold of her hand and lifted it to lightly kiss her knuckles, she sank back onto the cushions.

After a brief glance at her wedding ring, he asked, "Promise me you won't work too late?"

"I wish I could."

"Then at least move to my office where the light is better for your eyes."

"That I might do, thanks."

He gently squeezed her fingers, then, abruptly, let her go.

As she heard the engine of his vehicle start, she sighed. He'd been the epitome of a perfect gentleman— exactly what she'd hoped he would be. But that was only partially true.

Chapter Seven

To keep her thoughts from lingering too long on what-ifs, E.D. plucked up her cell phone from the coffee table. It was dusk and the phone lit brightly as she keyed the phone book. Reasoning that with her troubles stacked high, Dani would be entombed in her room as Mac had said, miserable and lonely; maybe, just maybe, her daughter might be willing to finally pick up the call.

After several rings, Dani did. But her first words were hardly encouraging. "You're not supposed to contact me."

Her accusatory tone had E.D. immediately checking her own responses. "You're my daughter, Dani. I can't let a piece of paper, won under false pretenses, intimidate me. If you want to call out to your father and report me, that's your right, but you should know, he's likely to file with the police, who will put out a warrant to arrest me. Is that what you want?"

Her gentle, reasonable approach brought silence. E.D. took hope in that—at least the teen hadn't hung up.

"He's not here anyway."

On a Saturday night with the media skulking around? "Is he at the market or getting takeout for dinner?"

"I don't know. I only heard the garage door open and close."

Without warning her or Mac that he was leaving? What on earth…? "Have you eaten?"

"I'm not hungry."

"That's understandable," E.D. replied with hard-learned patience. "Even so, you need to consider your health. Want me to order a pizza to the house? You love Canadian bacon and pineapple. What about Mac? Do you want to go ask what kind he wants?"

"He won't eat it. He doesn't feel well."

Dread was like a lead weight on her chest. "Did he have another attack?"

"It's just a virus he picked up at school. Now I'll probably get all the dumping on me because I checked on him and told. What was I supposed to do with no one else around who cares?"

Normally, E.D. would quietly but firmly chide her daughter for her martyr theatrics—which increasingly resembled some of Trey's worst personality traits—but she knew that would be a shortcut to being disconnected. As unpalatable and disappointing as this was, it was all she had to work with at the moment. "I know you've always been protective of your brother, Dani, and I'm proud of you for that. Maybe your dad went to get something for him at the pharmacy. I'm sure he'll be right back."

"Yeah, right. He's been gone over an hour already."

Good grief! Their pharmacy was three blocks from the house. What was going on? If there had been a wait at the pharmacy, or an accident, he should have called for backup to make sure the kids were okay. While E.D. struggled to control her breathing, she tried to think of what to say.

"Mac said he saw you earlier today," Dani continued, her irritation unchecked. "He said Dad was seriously ticked."

"Did your father say anything to you?"

"Is that all you think about? How to either defend yourself or get back at him? If you cared so much, why didn't you come here to see me while they were gone?"

Ah, now there was the exposing comment, E.D. thought without pleasure. "Would you have welcomed that? Do you realize that if I'd risked it, the neighbors would probably have relayed as much to your father and he could have me sitting in jail as we speak?"

"You risked getting arrested for Mac."

"Not much of a risk—your father doesn't care for chess. Even so, it turned out badly, as you obviously know. I thought it was my best chance to get a message to you and Mac. He apparently passed it on to you."

"Yeah, yeah. The truth is that you chose him because he hasn't tarnished your precious reputation."

E.D. rubbed at her forehead, stunned that her first-born thought pointing fingers and making wild accusations would get her the sympathy she thought she deserved, instead of taking responsibility for her actions. "Things are going to continue being pretty bleak for you if you refuse to take a different route than this one," she told her. "And it would help if you remember I have tried to call you."

"What for—to listen to this? It's hard enough that my father is calling me a tramp and I'm the joke of the decade at school," Dani wailed. "I expected you to get it right. You've had the free ride until now!"

What on earth…? E.D. forced herself to refrain from responding immediately, but her thoughts raced. Trey must've been filling her ears for some time for her to summon such a low blow this easily. A free ride regarding what? She was the chief income earner—the sole income earner—in the family, and she strove to come home every night and participate; ask for news and achievements; commiserate or offer advice when and where it was needed. Dani hadn't only hurt her, she'd insulted her.

Swallowing her pride, E.D. began, "I promise you, I am wading chest deep here and clueless as to my free ride. Can you give me specifics and details?"

"Oh, my God!" the girl shouted. "My life is ruined and all you care about is saving your own butt?"

"Dani!"

"I hate you!"

E.D. heard that unmistakable beep that signaled Dani had disconnected.

Shaking from shock as much as outrage, it took two tries to turn off her phone. Rising, she paced the length of the room and back again trying to make reason out of what she'd just heard. She knew better than to believe her daughter's anger was wholly and fairly directed at her; nevertheless, words took their toll. So upset was she that she didn't hear the vehicle outside and barely registered the single knock at the door before Dylan re-entered.

"Sorry to disturb, I forgot to pick up the grill's empty propane tank and—" belatedly Dylan noted E.D.'s stricken expression "—what is it?"

Truth be known, he couldn't resist stopping by again. The check-in with Chris had gone quickly, and he'd been loath to take any more of his friend and employee's weekend than necessary. Also Dylan had been eager to have a last few minutes with E.D. because any way he looked at it, the next week was going to be long and lonely.

"I just hung up with Dani," she said.

"She called?"

"No, I broke down and did…and wish I hadn't. She hates me and thinks I've had a free ride. Through what I don't know." E.D. lifted her arms in helpless defeat. "My marriage? Her making terrible decisions? I don't get any of this."

Cursing his promise to keep his distance, Dylan crossed to her to take her into his arms. "It sounds like you have to install a better filter. With your caseload and what else is bound to come down the transom, you can't take anything she says to heart."

E.D. rocked her forehead against his shoulder and

yet he saw her hands were fisted against his chest as though fighting for control. He knew strong people like her didn't handle protectiveness well; they were used to providing the protection.

"I'm working on it. Motherhood is wrestling with the veteran prosecutor, though. What in the world has Trey or anyone else filled her head with? Don't answer that," she added, disengaging herself to pace.

The only reason Dylan let her go was that she was clearly working through something. He wanted to be allowed to hang around and help.

"There is some good news in all of this," she announced.

Dylan leaned back against the back of a couch and crossed his arms. "You've got my undivided attention."

"It didn't register with me until she'd disconnected. Get this—Trey didn't sign my name to the papers."

Not knowing how she could be certain, he ventured, "She came right out and said that and put all the blame on you?"

"I doubt she ever realized what she'd said. *But* she confessed how furious her father was with her. To quote her, he called her a tramp."

Wondering at the sudden light in her eyes, Dylan's gaze settled on the coffee he'd made for her on the table. It remained almost untouched. "Why don't I warm that up and make myself some, and you can explain that."

E.D. followed him to the kitchen. "You don't see? What this could mean?"

"You get your family back once everything is resolved."

He went on to the kitchen fully aware that she would follow him like a drone missile streaking after its target. As he reached for the coffeepot, she stayed his hand.

"Why would you think that...and in that disapproving way?"

Disapproving? Dylan decided she was being too generous. More like jealous, petty and selfish.

Slowly forcing him to face her until she could meet his gaze, she shook her head. "You're so good. You won't even say anything that might influence what you think is my right to my own decision."

"Don't be so sure." Wrapping his left arm around her waist, he swept her close, cupped his right hand at the back of her head to keep her still and locked his mouth over hers. What did he have to lose? She'd just shocked him into realizing how standing back and waiting patiently can land you at the end of the road—or your dream—so alone that it wouldn't even be worth taking another breath.

There was no tentativeness this time; he kissed her with unrestrained passion, making it clear how deep his hunger went. He wanted hours of just that. She was the ultimate enigma to him—visually elegant and reserved, but beneath was a woman of many layers to be discovered. For better or worse, in each life some irresistible something or someone appeared to mark a crossroads—E.D. was his.

When he lifted his head he had to suck in much-needed air before acceding, "Fine. He's innocent. He still doesn't get you back."

E.D. blinked. "No, he doesn't."

But the look she gave him told him she would decide her future. Nobody else. "Glad we agree on something."

"Dylan—"

He backed away immediately, his hands in the air. "I'm behaving." Reaching for her mug, he put it into the microwave and punched in an adequate heating time, then reached for a mug for himself.

"I didn't say Trey is innocent of everything," E.D. said to his back. "Just forgery. And that's an educated and hopeful guess, nothing conclusive."

"Hopeful."

"As in 'I'd like nothing more than to be able to get this ugly story resolved before I become one of the late-night talk shows' top ten news topics of the year.'" E.D. moved to his side to study his profile. "That doesn't explain or excuse a number of other offenses committed by Trey. All I'm saying is it's likely my daughter did more than betray my trust, Dylan. My kid, for all I tried to teach her, is apparently gifted in deceit and who knows what else?"

Dylan zeroed in on her necessity to take blame again. "Okay, so you won't make mentor of the year. What you should be focusing on is that Trey *is* in the guardianship role and he sure doesn't seem to have lost much sleep over any of this. That said, regardless of parental input, Dani is, in the end, her own person and damned close to legal age." He thought it wise to resist adding that the girl was abusing the right thoroughly.

"It doesn't sound like you need caffeine any more than I do," she murmured.

"No."

"All I wanted to share is that my daughter is upset that her father is angry with her, indicating that there is no collusion—at least where permission slips are concerned."

Dylan nodded, thinking that through. "This is good news?"

"Probably not. It will require deeper digging, but on a family level it gives me...oxygen."

There was that family inference again. "Oxygen?"

"The key, Dylan," she whispered with renewed hope, "the key is that my daughter doesn't understand her father's anger, and my husband thinks I have done something reckless and unprofessional. There's something outside the family dynamics working here."

He nodded and was relieved to see her sounding stronger. But he felt strangely outside of whatever sphere she was in.

"That doesn't shut you out," she said softly. "The fact is I don't think I could have gotten even this far without you."

Despite his pounding heart, he merely nodded again. "I'm just a call away."

Chapter Eight

The next several days passed in a blur thanks to already tight schedules, kinks in plans and surprises. By Thursday, E.D. had spoken with Alyx and Ivan no less than a dozen times while dealing with her own load of cases. She'd made innumerable notes, filled out form after form, and was preparing for a first face-to-face with Trey and his attorney. None of that mattered due to her concern about the progress that Ivan Priestly was making. The problem was the last two times she had called on Friday morning, his assistant had hurriedly taken her name and promised a call back.

"Shouldn't you be in court?"

It was nearing ten o'clock as E.D. exited her office and ran into Emmett and his clerk.

"Defense asked for a two-hour delay. Their client got

into a fight with his cot and needed emergency medical care this morning."

With his usual aplomb, the D.A. merely cocked an eyebrow and slowed his stride to match hers. "How unfortunate that the cot wasn't stronger. There's no telling what a benefit it might have served the taxpayer." He cast her a sidelong look. "And you? How goes it on the home front?"

She wasn't about to expose anything while his latest ambitious pup was right on their heels listening, even if his eyes were discreetly focused on the tweed carpet. "We've gone to jury for the Herrera case," she replied, intentionally misunderstanding him.

Without missing a beat, Emmett asked, "I trust you're comfortable with that?"

It was the least publicized of her cases because everyone expected him to be convicted. "If worse comes to worst, I have notes ready to get transcribed for Appeals. The police did an impeccable job with evidence, sir. He'll go down."

"I believe that, as well."

E.D. relaxed somewhat knowing that if he'd had any serious reservations, he'd readily have dogged her. With that narrow corridor to breathe, she stood back from the two men at the elevators. While Emmett's clerk pushed the button, Emmett crooned, "I'm sorry I'm forcing you to burn the midnight oil at this difficult time."

Sure he was, E.D. thought, praying for the car's speedy arrival. She managed a nod, but just as the elevator dinged its arrival, her phone buzzed. She quickly plucked the cell from her pocket and saw the caller was Dylan.

"Yes?" she said into the mouthpiece.

As Emmett stepped inside the car, E.D. hesitated. "Uh, sir, go on ahead. I have to pick up a fax at my office.

"Thank you, cavalry," she muttered, retracing her steps down the hall. Intermittently glancing around her, she paused to open her door. "You still there?"

"Did I recognize Emmett's voice?" Dylan asked.

"The one and only."

"Sorry. I wouldn't have intruded if this wasn't important."

Meaning he had bad news. That deduction, backed up by his grim tone had E.D. steeling herself for the worst. "Tell me."

"It's Ivan. He's suffered a heart attack."

Entering her office, she closed the door behind her with soundless precision. Then she slumped back against it. "Dear Lord." Inevitably, her mind went into overdrive; she envisioned Ivan's sweet elfin face with his shrewd eyes and wild eyebrows; following that came the realization of what this did to her case. Was Dylan about to break even worse news to her? "Oh, please. Tell me he isn't…?"

"He's holding his own. Hell, I don't know. I'm awaiting word on the severity of the attack and his prognosis."

"How did you find out in the first place?"

"Don't ask, not on this phone. You know our society is small and the inner circles smaller. I'm sorry about this, the timing stinks. Are you all right?"

The concern in his voice was endearing, almost as

reassuring as being in strong arms. "Never mind me, that poor man. What can I do? I have to be in court in twenty minutes, but tell me is there anything? Anyone I should contact?"

"Phone Alyx before you go into court and get stuck in there for hours. She needs the heads-up—and she might be able to come up with a strong replacement."

What was she, a day-care teacher? "I can—"

"You're tied up."

"Of course." Trying not to let the new tension get to her, E.D. added, "If you find out more about his condition, will you leave a message on my cell?"

"You know I will. Let *me* know if you get out earlier than expected. I can pick up dinner and feed you while you work."

"I will—unless Alyx needs to meet with me."

"Then call and let me know what she said."

"If it's not too late."

"The time doesn't matter."

Smiling at the caress he always put in his closing words, she murmured, "Bye," and disconnected. The smile became a worried frown by the time she keyed Alyx's number.

Dylan had just exited the elevator when he spotted a familiar face across the marble-floored lobby of the courthouse. "Jonas."

Jonas Hunter glanced around, his trim athlete's body pivoting smoothly. "Judge." His studious expression relaxed into one of wry pleasure as he drew nearer and extended his hand. "How are you, Dylan?"

It had been amusing to hear his old friend use the formal greeting for other ears when they had once been young Turks competing for the best grades at UT and weekend competitors at the gym. They used to reduce each other to a sweat slick on the racquetball court—and every court available—while calling each other far more casual names.

"Fine, fine." Dylan patted the inches-shorter man on the shoulder with his free hand. "Good to see you. Why the heck didn't you call and let me know you'd be in town? We could have arranged something."

"I wasn't sure how busy things would be until today. I flew in to testify on an old case that had been pushed back so often I thought I'd be retired or the accused would die of old age before we made it to court."

"Where's home now?"

Jonas exhaled with weariness. "The cradle of our nation, better known as the Beltway, which is the more appropriate appellation considering how many hours we all sit in traffic." He suddenly frowned. "Hey, I'm sorry about Brenda. I was asking the judge in my case about you yesterday and he told me that she'd lost her battle with cancer. I was out of the country when it happened, otherwise—"

"It's all right," Dylan interjected and gripped his arm. "Thanks, though. It was a relief for her."

With a tight-lipped nod, Jonas studied him. "Then I'm grateful for both of you. Are you by chance free? Can you afford to be seen drinking beer in public? I've only just heard about your plans. We need to celebrate before I'm too lowly to claim any acquaintance."

"You need to get out of Washington," Dylan drawled to the blue-eyed man whose ash-blond hair was beginning to turn prematurely silver. "You're beginning to sound like a veteran politician." He was about to beg off when it struck him that this was the perfect opportunity to get some advice for E.D. "The step up is a humble hope, but thanks. Why don't you follow me to my place? It's only blocks from here. If you have the time I'd like to pick your brain on a matter on behalf of an associate."

"Is she redheaded with legs up to here?" Jonas drawled, his eyes twinkling as he sliced his hand across his neck.

"Actually, she's blond and looks like Cheryl Ladd's kid sister."

Tilting his head, Jonas's expression grew respectful. "Count me in, old son. Where do you big shots park?"

Fifteen minutes later they were shedding their suit jackets in Dylan's condo and he went for the bar refrigerator. "The usual?"

"That will hit the spot. Thanks."

He grabbed two bottles of Heineken and circled the bar to where Jonas was pulling at the tie that matched his silvery-blue eyes. Also in his early forties, Jonas had always drawn female eyes; aside from his commercial good looks, some physical energy emanated around him that suggested he was a prowling predator ready to pounce. Dylan did notice there were the inevitable signs on his face, particularly around his eyes and mouth, that indicated devoting oneself to a mentally and emotionally demanding job took its toll.

"Forgive me for not asking sooner," he said, handing over one of the beers, "how're Claudia and Blake?"

Accepting the green bottle, Jonas took a moment to focus on opening it. "Claudia and I split two years ago."

At first, Dylan didn't know what to say. He'd never seen the two as a good match: Claudia was a high-maintenance woman, all about being seen with the right people at the right places; Jonas was most at home sleeping by a campfire or settling for a cold hot dog to avoid missing a fast-moving ballgame moment. Still, when kids were involved, that was hardly anything compared to, say, E.D.'s situation.

"How's Blake taking that?" he asked.

"Heck, he's thirteen and has hardly noticed. He's torn between body piercings and starting his own software company. Even with my hand in computer forensics, I feel like a novice watching him."

"Two years—has Claudia remarried?"

"She was a June bride, so she's almost celebrating her first anniversary. She's moving up in the world—he's a polo player with his own team."

"Ah. Success at last."

Jonas laughed easily. "I can't tell you how grateful I am to him. We were living in an alimony state."

"Yeah, but just think—if you'd held on to her, you might have become director of the FBI. Her daddy still has clout, doesn't he?" Dylan gestured to the leather chairs by the fireplace.

With a faked shudder, Jonas settled into the one on the left. "There's another gratifying escape. I like to be in the thick of things too much for people like him. You would have been his pick. You're a natural leader, the one to change perspective with words. I'm only on the right side of the courtroom because the Bureau keeps my brain interested and my gun license current."

He'd always been like that, underplaying his intelligence and hiding his heart. "You're still full of it, Hunter, and I'm damned glad to see you haven't changed."

Jonas took a swallow of his beer. "So what's got you going against the grain and willing to talk about personal business in light of what's pending for you?"

"Fate…good or bad timing, depending how you look at it. An exceptional woman in a tough situation that she doesn't deserve." Dylan summarized the story about E.D.'s daughter and the latest news about Ivan. "As you can see there's been a streak of bad luck."

"Any more and I'd make the sign of the cross and get the heck out of here for fear of catching some of it." Jonas took another swallow of beer. "Talk about bad timing, need I mention that you shouldn't be seen as tied to this even innocently, my friend?"

"Understood. I also know that if asked to choose between damaging my career chances forever, and being here for E.D., it wouldn't take two seconds to decide."

Jonas whistled silently as he stared at his bottle's label. "Have you told the governor?"

With a droll look, Dylan asked, "What do you think? Either I'm in or I'm out. As of this moment, there's no need to be out."

"I agree," Jonas said, "but what about interviews? Background investigations?"

"Unless someone is listening to my calls, no one

knows about her yet. She prefers it that way and is trying to keep me at arm's length and not let me do something foolish."

"Sounds like a smart woman. You should listen to her."

"Damn it, Jonas, she's an election away from being the next D.A., her record is that impressive and unimpeachable."

"And you're one of the good guys, too, and critical to the big picture. Good God, I may be sitting across from the future governor…or a supreme court judge."

Dylan sat forward. "None of which matters if I'm making the journey alone." He leaned forward, his elbows on his knees. "I have stood on the sidelines for longer than I want to admit watching her…and wanting."

Jonas looked away. "I don't know whether to feel sorry for you or envious as hell." Polishing off the last of his beer, he set it on the table between them and took out a small notebook from his jacket pocket. "First thing we need to do is shut down that Web site. I can't believe E.D.'s husband didn't contact us before he got busy getting rid of her. The damage is done now and those photos will be all over the Internet—potentially forever. If you knew how many sites there are like that, you'd lose that beer, especially if you saw how many include minors and worse yet babies.

"Why didn't E.D. go to the police and turn in the guy the moment she found out? Even with the signed authorization implicating her, the girl's a minor."

"This exploded in her face all of nine days ago and she didn't know which photographer, and was cut off from contacting her daughter for the information. Believe me, she's doing what she can behind the scenes while trying to appease her ambitious boss, who as I explained plans to run for governor in the next election and doesn't want anything like this situation besmirching his image." Dylan pinched the bridge of his nose. "All this while trying to deal with a worm of a husband."

"Can you set it up for me to meet with your lady? I need whatever details she can give me. Shutting down the site won't be a problem—hell, my kid's a better hacker than some of the people in our office—but I'll need to speak with the district office here and get their people officially on the case."

Dylan rose to get his phone. "I'm sorry for what's undoubtedly going to eat up your free time."

"Are you kidding? You're about to save me from too many hours in a motel room," Jonas said with a grin.

Chapter Nine

"I had you scheduled for a meeting next Tuesday with Trey and his attorney," Alyx said to E.D. "But considering the news about Ivan, you might want me to push that back."

E.D. stood at the window of Alyx's modern glass-and-chrome office and immediately turned her back on her tenth-floor view of Austin. "Please, no. I don't know when I'll have another free block of time this size."

Alyx slapped E.D.'s file onto her desk. "Then let me put this another way—you're stretched too thin even for my needs of your time. Juggling your caseload, a delicate divorce, and now working with the FBI is bound to have you stumbling somewhere. Don't think Trey—or rather his attorney—won't be salivating for that moment."

"Trey can have anything he wants as long as he'll let me have my kids," E.D. replied.

"Oh, thanks," Alyx groaned reaching for her head. "I really needed to hear that."

Fortunately, the phone rang, giving E.D. a momentary reprieve from what Alyx planned to volley back at that admission. Facing the window again, she hoped she wasn't making the world's biggest mistake. So much hung on Dylan, his request that she trust him, and the mystery friend he was bringing to the meeting.

Within seconds of arriving at Alyx's office, Dylan had rung on her cell phone. He'd made short work of explaining why he was interrupting and Alyx—with surprising support—had immediately sent her remaining staffers home for the day to protect the identity of E.D.'s "guests." The fewer people who saw one of the state's more powerful people and a FBI agent in the same meeting as her newsworthy client the better was how she'd put it. But that didn't mean the lady litigator was happy with this infringement on her time and space despite E.D. swearing that she hadn't known about Agent Hunter until the call.

If Alyx was furious with her for not telling her about Dylan, she had company. E.D. wasn't happy with any of this, either, and Alyx would have to take a backseat to her anger if this turned into a disaster of an idea.

Massaging the pain growing between her eyebrows, E.D. was surprised to feel a nudge. Alyx stood beside her with two white pills and a bottle of water. E.D. knew she was definitely slipping; she hadn't heard her end her call, let alone move around the office. Murmuring her thanks, she downed the pills and two sips of water.

"Bless you for that," she told the other woman. "I hope these work in record time."

She liked as well as admired Alyx. The woman was a force to be reckoned with—exotic and stunning with a razor-sharp mind that rarely exhibited any sign of weakness. E.D. thought she looked fairly pulled together in her Wedgwood-blue coatdress, but Alyx in her black silk designer suit made her feel like a lady-in-waiting to a queen.

"Don't study me with those limpid doe eyes, damn it," Alyx snapped. "If you weren't already hurting, I'd shake you until your back teeth were loose. Judge Justiss! For crying out loud, are you suicidal?"

"I told you, we're old friends. I've known him since I was in college."

"Sure, I used to play in the sandbox behind the White House with Ronald Reagan's kids. Are you having an affair? Stupid question," she scoffed. "I only have to say his name and your color rises, you, you *blonde*." Alyx pointed a well-manicured, fiery-red fingernail at her. "You'd better pray this bit of news stays out of the press or you'll be found guilty in the public's eye before your husband's attorney poses the first question during depositions."

A knock at the door saved E.D. from having to apologize. Alyx glanced over her shoulder.

"Come in!" she snapped.

Dylan entered, behind him an attractive man dressed in the conservative style that spoke of government. E.D.

inspected him only long enough to be certain she knew his tailoring concealed a weapon, then couldn't help a rush of joy as Dylan's dark blue gaze lasered into hers. It felt almost as intimate as being in his arms.

With a low sound of disgust, Alyx muttered to her, "I rest my case." Then she crossed the carpet and extended her hand. "Judge, it's an honor. I'm Alyx Carmel."

"I've heard many good things about you, Ms. Carmel. This is Special Agent Hunter with the FBI."

"Make that Jonas, please," Jonas said as he shook hands with Alyx. "Especially since I'm not here in an official capacity." *Yet* hung in the air like the fading gong of a bell.

His smile came quickly, though, and E.D. noticed his eyes lit with male appreciation as his gaze roamed over her attorney's face. She also took in with growing interest that the handshake lasted perhaps a second or two longer than professional politeness dictated.

But even as the impulse to smile pulled at her lips, Jonas was crossing to her. "Mrs. Sessions—"

"Ms. Martel." She could see from his shrewd gaze that he already knew that and was somehow testing her. "I'd be happier if you'd simply make it E.D.," she said quietly.

Something gentled in his expression. "I'd be delighted, although there's nothing simple about that, is there?"

"Excuse me, gentlemen," Alyx announced, "please make yourself comfortable while I lock the exterior door to the suite."

E.D. exchanged looks with Dylan again. They'd briefly discussed Alyx's security problem.

"I noticed the squad car sitting outside the building and the security guard was considerably thorough in checking our ID," he said, stepping closer. "Nothing's changed?"

"I'm afraid not," E.D. replied with the same courtroom whisper. "She's being remarkably calm. I'd be a basket case." E.D. could tell by Jonas's lack of expression that he'd been filled in about the need for caution.

"You're a mother," Dylan countered. "The danger would be compounded in your case."

His defense of her was both endearing and embarrassing considering that they were hardly alone. She quickly turned to Jonas. "I'm grateful for your willingness to offer some input…Jonas. I understand your time is precious."

"Hardly that bad. I hope I can be of service, and I'm sorry for your troubles."

E.D. liked him more with every minute. "You and Dylan go back some years I understand?"

"Far enough that I can torture him with stories about whipping his butt on the racquetball court."

"And I get to pay him back reminding him of dates lost due to his day job," Dylan returned with good humor.

E.D. smiled. "Oh, dear. That sounds like a draw."

"Is everyone ready to begin?" Alyx asked crisply as she returned.

She'd undoubtedly heard that exchange and appeared unamused by it. E.D. glanced at Dylan and caught his conspiratorial wink. Yes, she thought, Jonas was a definite flirt, and Alyx was pretending not to be attracted.

"Can I get anyone anything?" When they all declined, Alyx gestured to the sitting area with the cranberry leather couch and two navy-blue chairs framing a glass coffee table. "Then since this is out of my area of expertise, Agent Hunter—"

"Jonas."

"—why don't you ask what it is you need to know and what you think you can do for my client?"

"I plan to clean up the Internet a little," Jonas said with a meaningful nod to E.D. "And then I hope to aid you in identifying who's behind all of this. Also to find out why Mr. Sessions didn't contact us immediately upon learning his daughter was compromised."

Two hours later, E.D. exited the building with the others and, as the security guard locked up after them, Alyx waved to the police officer waiting in his patrol car. E.D. repressed a shiver and thanked the brunette again for being so understanding. Then she shook hands with Jonas.

"It was a pleasure to meet you," she said with growing respect.

"Same here. I hope to be able to ease your mind soon."

When E.D. turned to Dylan, he said immediately, "I'm following you home. No arguments. This is for my peace of mind."

Self-conscious, she glanced at Jonas and Alyx.

"Smart idea," Jonas said with a nod of approval.

"Do you need a lift, Agent Hunter?" Alyx asked coolly.

"I've got a rental, thanks. But I would like to ask you about—"

As Jonas and Alyx focused on each other, E.D. escaped to her pearl-white Mercedes.

She couldn't deny a feeling of reassurance at seeing Dylan's SUV's headlights in her rearview mirror as she turned onto the road. It was fast approaching dusk and would be quite dark by the time they reached the ranch. Too, her mind was whirling from Jonas Hunter's grim statistics about the pervasiveness of child pornography in the world today. She knew it was bad, but had had no idea of the specifics. His assurance that, despite the humiliation of the costly experience, Dani's case wasn't nearly as bad as some he'd dealt with gave E.D. hope. Maybe her daughter's life wouldn't be ruined forever.

After a deep breath, E.D. reached for her cell phone and briefly checked on Ivan's condition. An attendant at the nurses' station informed her that he was in stable condition, his prognosis good. His son happened to be passing by and recognized her name. He took the phone and warmly relayed a message of regret from his father. Dear Ivan, she thought once she hung up. To worry about a client at a time like this.

It was a relief to drive through the electronic gates of the ranch. A feeling of homecoming warmed her like a sip of cognac. Except for missing her children, the moment would have been perfect. It also struck her as interesting that until Jonas had brought up his name, she hadn't thought of Trey once all day.

As she parked, she felt a strong tide of transition carry her to a new perspective. Perhaps the fact that Alyx and Jonas had now seen her and Dylan together made it possible for her to openly acknowledge there was something between them? Or was it having verbalized Trey's conduct that was finally freeing her from feeling she was still tied more than legally to him?

Shutting down the engine, she caught sight of her wedding band, a simple weave of yellow and white gold. She'd never had an engagement ring and hadn't been hurt at the time when Trey had apologized for not being able to afford one. She'd thought herself in love, but realized she'd been a fool.

Slipping off the ring, she dropped it into her purse.

Dylan came to open her car door and since her hands were full with her bag and briefcase, he quickly jostled his keys to get the right one into the house door. "That was a nice drive, not one other vehicle on the road— and on a Friday night no less. I should have taken the lead," he added. "Then my headlights wouldn't have been constantly in your rearview mirror."

"Sure, but then you'd be a driving hazard because you'd be constantly checking *your* mirror," E.D. teased.

Pushing the door wide for her, he smiled. "Guilty."

E.D. shook her head at his unabashed frankness and continued inside where she dropped her purse and briefcase onto the couch. It was a pleasure to be free of their weight. So was slipping off her sling-back high heels.

"Are you hungry?" Dylan asked, closing and locking the door. "I should have thought to suggest takeout, but I can make—"

"Oh, nothing for me, thanks," she interjected. "I think my stomach is still trying to handle the grilled-chicken salad I had for lunch. Don't let me stop you, though." It undoubtedly took a man of his size a solid three meals a day to maintain his strength and health.

She'd left enough timed night-lights on in the house to make navigation easy, so when Dylan reached for the main light switch, she begged him not to. "I'm tired of light and the sounds of the city. This is perfect."

"It is that. How about a glass of wine?"

She murmured her thanks even though she didn't really think she wanted that, either; nevertheless, as he headed for the kitchen, she welcomed the extra moment to shed the last vestiges of what had been the second most demanding day since this had all begun. Slipping off the antique gold chain with the ornate onyx-and-gold pendant inherited from a beloved aunt, and the matching earrings, she set them all on the coffee table; then removed the pins from her chignon. Dropping them into her pocket, she followed Dylan while massaging her aching neck.

He was pouring the red wine they'd opened last weekend. As he handed her one of the goblets, he gave her a slow, sweeping inspection aided by the illumination from the floodlights off the back patio. "After all the hours you've put in today, how do you manage to continue looking like you do?"

The unveiled emotions in his eyes had E.D. swallowing against a dry throat. "The other benefit of strategically low lighting," she said, opting for humor before lifting the glass to her lips.

Protesting her self-deprecation with a rumble from deep in his chest, Dylan sipped, too. "You're not mad at me for bringing in Jonas?"

As the essence of the liquor permeated her senses, she reached up and stroked his cheek, letting her thumb caress the strong line of his jaw, the beginnings of a five o'clock shadow. "No. I was, admittedly, concerned at first, but I should have known you were doing the right thing for Dani."

"Mostly for you."

"In the end, it's the same thing. You were trying to protect us from things getting worse."

His broad chest rose and fell on a long breath. "Thank you for that understanding, and trust." He took hold of the hand that had caressed him and brought it over his heart.

"Jonas, for all of his machismo, seems a capable man, and yet I think he admires you very much."

Dylan's eyes lit with mischievous pleasure. "He's eaten with jealousy. He thinks you're a knockout, not to mention quite the lady. I could tell."

E.D. dismissed that with a brief shake of her head and pointed at him with her glass. "His focus is on Alyx and I'll wager they're together right now."

"Nah. Alyx is a comely barracuda. Jonas isn't the type to trade one carnivore for another."

"You saw how long that initial handshake lasted," E.D. said with equal amusement.

"That was Jonas being Jonas. He's a born flirt and adores women. If he'd been seriously interested in her, he wouldn't have admitted to having his rental there and let her drive him back to his hotel."

Again, E.D. rejected that approach. "He read her perfectly and knew she would be annoyed to discover any kind of manipulation or game playing. That's why he went after her to ask one more question—which is, I promise you, an invitation for a drink if not dinner."

"And that maneuver wouldn't be game playing?"

"No, that's an initial step in the mating dance."

Dylan's eyes grew serious. "I want to dance with you."

"Now who's the flirt?"

Instead of answering, his gaze dropped to the hand he continued to hold. He'd been stroking her fingers with his thumb and frowned as he obviously realized that she no longer wore her ring. Putting down his glass, he then took hers and set it on the counter, too. Slowly taking her into his arms, he searched her eyes. "I'm not flirting, and I've never been more serous in my life. But I need to know something. In Alyx's office, you were still wearing your wedding band—and now you're not. What's changed?"

"I realized as we drove in here that I was coming home," she said, her confidence growing thanks to his perception. "That I'd been wearing the ring out of habit and for no other reason. That maybe I'd been using it to keep you at arm's length, and that I needed to stop being a coward."

"You're no coward. You're just inundated with responsibility and priorities. What do *you* want, E.D.?"

She reached up to draw his head down to hers and whispered against his lips, "You."

With a brief murmur of relief or approval, Dylan tightened his arms and claimed her lips with his. E.D. inched closer, loving his strength and size. It had been several days since he'd last kissed her, and he was what she'd been craving, not the wine. Her thirst was for him—his taste, his touch and his presence. Although they'd talked every day on the phone—sometimes three or four times—she'd missed actually seeing him. She shared how much in her avid response to his probing kiss, in the tightening of her arms, and in the way she pressed closer to fit her body more perfectly against his.

With a low moan, he lifted her against him so that her body cupped his growing arousal. That intimacy proved as erotic as the dream she'd wakened from this morning. There was no impatience; desire in its purest wasn't about selfishness, but an outward focus to experience the realm of sensations, as well as each iota of nuance.

It was Dylan who ended the kiss, and in a most sensual way, sliding his mouth across her cheek and down her neck where his steamy, not quite steady sigh dampened her skin. Slowly, he lowered her to the floor. E.D. was grateful he didn't release her; she wasn't sure her legs would obey any command from her brain, conscious or automatic, to stay standing.

Without a word, he took her hand and led her out of the kitchen and down the hall. E.D. went, knowing in that instant that she would have followed him into the ocean or off the edge of the world.

Just inside the doorway of the bedroom, he stepped aside for her to enter. When she did, he slipped his arm around her waist and drew her back against his chest. E.D. understood that he was giving her one last chance to change her mind and to be sure this was what she wanted.

She wouldn't.

It was.

He was.

As he buried his face in her hair, whispering some unintelligible endearment or accolade, she pressed her bottom against his hips and drew his left hand to her right breast, his other hand to palm her mound. His touch sent a long-repressed hunger through her and her body's reaction was of frissons surging through her. Gasping, she dropped her head back against his shoulder and absorbed each delicious sensation.

Dylan took full advantage and pressed his lips to her neck, scored the slender tendons with his teeth, suckling gently, but with an ardor that promised he would be compelled to leave marks elsewhere.

Afraid she would lose control before they were even undressed, E.D. took hold of one too-gifted hand and drew him to the side of the bed where she began sliding off his jacket. His gaze wholly on her, Dylan made short work of his tie, then the two of them dealt with his shirt buttons. The regular gym workouts and all the physical labor here on the ranch were evidenced as his strong, well-toned body was slowly exposed—a wholly different specimen of the man hidden behind those robes. She'd guessed as much, but was glad never to have had her suspicions proven until now. What an impossible temptation he would have been if she had known.

"What's that impish smile for?" he asked, breaking into her thoughts.

"I was thinking of all the women in your court who

would need to wipe the drool from their chins if they saw you this way." Still smiling, she reached for his belt buckle.

"Well, I'm not about to think of anyone seeing you this way," he replied, undoing the gold buttons of her dress.

He always managed to say the right thing. Unable to speak her gratitude, E.D. leaned forward and pressed a kiss to his heart, then turned to bestow a lick and nip to his left nipple. Dylan sucked in a sharp breath; a second later, he buried his hands in her hair. The silent request had her repeating the caress.

Lifting her gaze to meet his, she murmured, "I want you."

"I need you," he replied seeking her mouth.

By the end of the next ardent kiss, he'd finished undressing her. Then they stepped from the silk, cotton and nylon puddled around them and stretched onto the bed.

"Beautiful Eva Danielle." He stroked her from shoulder to thigh and explored everywhere in between.

Sliding her hand over his hip, she urged him closer until his full, hot length was between her thighs. "I can't wait to feel you, just you, inside me."

Intent on worshipping, Dylan made her wait. His hands were gifted, his mouth a treasure. When she finally closed her fingers around him, he thrust into her hand and sighed into her mouth, "Take me home, Eva Danielle."

Nothing else he could have said would have been more perfect. She whispered his name and drew him over her.

His entrance was smooth and complete. Drinking in her gasp, he kept still when she trembled. "Okay?"

She didn't have the voice to tell him that her response wasn't about weight or pain, rather the awe of feelings never before experienced. She could only wrap her legs around him and hold him tighter.

Once again Dylan's instincts were on target; he reassured, navigated their way through the forces driving them both. It had been so long since she'd let her feminine side surface that a part of E.D. resisted the flood of emotions and sensations rushing through her. Dylan's passion permeated her defenses, vanquishing the ghost of who she'd been and where she'd been hiding, filling every pore and cell with life and the hunger for it.

She reached for it, and him.

Dylan resisted moving, certain that if he did, what they'd just shared might prove to be a dream. Only the worry that he was too heavy had him finally rolling onto his back.

To his surprise, E.D. immediately reached for him. "Dylan—don't leave."

"I'm not going anywhere, sweetheart." The thought of waking in the morning and seeing her beside him made his heart soar and when she slid over to snuggle against him, he gratefully tucked her closer. Pressing a kiss to her temple, he breathed in the scent of her hair. "Are lilies of the valley in season?"

"No, but you're amazing to recall it's my favorite scent. I remember you asking way back when."

"Looking at you, it could have been yesterday."

Stretching to kiss him on the chin, she asked, "So it's true what you said about being attracted to me from the first?"

Dylan thought *finally* he could speak of it openly. "It was like getting a line drive right between the eyes." He remembered his stunned state and had been almost relieved to get back home to what was familiar and see Brenda's photo on the chest of drawers to ground him. But now the feeling had returned. The moment she'd put her hands on him, all the years had vanished and it was as if they were back to that first soul-shaking instant.

"I thought I felt you start," she ventured, "but then I told myself it was me." Her voice even carried the young, unsure note he remembered and thought so dear. "I wish I'd have followed my first instincts."

"Like the idea of awestruck coeds, do you?"

"Only second to ravishing D.A.'s who can't keep their hands off of me."

Her elegant, long-fingered hands were caressing his chest and, increasingly, he felt every stroke in his groin. He couldn't remember the last time he'd had two climaxes in one day, never mind in one hour.

"I love that I'm still trembling from having you inside me," E.D. whispered.

That provocative statement had Dylan lifting her over him. "I thought you were exhausted?"

"Could be that's why I'm talking without editing myself." She touched her lips to his. "You made me wish I wasn't on the Pill. For one crazy moment, I knew we would have made a baby."

Overwhelmed, humbled, Dylan could barely speak. "What's so crazy about that?" he finally managed to say, his throat sounding raspy to his own ears.

Her answering look was gentle and a little sad. "Timing has never been on our side. If it ever is…well, we may be past *that* time."

He couldn't believe her fatalism, not when they were finally stepping into the dream. Running his hands down her slender length, he affirmed, "No one seeing this body would believe you've already had two children."

She smiled. "You're so good for my ego."

"We're good for each other." Seeing she could feel the reason why, he eased himself back into her and heard her breath catch. Lifting her higher, he sought and found her left breast, wet then suckled her, thinking of her full with milk, imagining the chance to taste a drop of his child's nourishment. As she gasped and arched deeper into his mouth—the movement driving him deeper into her—he did it again, simultaneously initiating a rhythmic thrusting.

"Dylan…"

"Look at me."

When she did, he gripped her slim hips and urged her to ride him harder to match his thrusts. He could tell she knew what he was thinking, and wouldn't, couldn't give it reality with words. It didn't matter— her gaze stayed locked with his, and that was all that counted. He saw that as her eyes welled, as her fingers gripping his shoulders tightened.

"Please," she whispered.

For the rest of my life, he thought surging into her.

As she gasped, he drew her down and locked his mouth to hers. Drinking in her cry, he climaxed again.

Chapter Ten

"This is decadent."

On Saturday morning, wearing little more than a short aqua-blue silk robe, E.D. watched Dylan create a calorie-defiant and aromatic omelet. They'd slept until sunrise and then showered together, which had resulted in another unbelievable joining. If it wasn't for the workload waiting for her, along with the need to check her cell phone for messages, she could have willingly spent the day this way.

I'm in love with you.

The thought came sweet and pure as she considered Dylan's profile. He was also casually, comfortably dressed in an open shirt and jeans, which he kept in the bedroom closet. He looked every bit the rancher slumming. The romance of that had her smiling impishly.

"What? It's not too much. I'm starving."

Grinning, she stroked his back. "I suspect you are. You've already put in a physical day." As he made a grab for one end of her silk belt, she escaped by skirting around the kitchen's center island. "I'm going to check my phone messages."

"We're eating in thirty seconds."

"I'll beat you to the table."

She hurried to her purse for the phone, then quickly keyed the proper codes to retrieve her calls. Her lingering smile froze upon hearing the last of three messages. It was only twenty minutes old:

"Mom! Mom! Dani's in Emergency! She swallowed something! Mom, are you there?"

Her mind racing, her hands trembling, she depressed the digit that would ring her son's number, and started back to the kitchen to tell Dylan she couldn't stay.

Glancing up, he immediately turned off the stove. "What's wrong?"

"Mac rang me minutes ago. Dani's at Emergency. She's done something crazy. Mac," she said into the phone. "Sweetheart, what's happened?"

"I don't know. She went to dance class about an hour ago and the next thing we heard was Ms. Garza is at the hospital with her. What if she dies, Mom?"

Oh, God, what could she have taken? E.D.'s imagination went into overdrive. "Hang on, Mac. It'll be okay. Where are you, at the hospital?"

"No, Dad told me I had to stay put here at the house."

That man, E.D. fumed. "It's not good for you to be alone after such stress, you could have an attack. Call

Mrs. Hobbs and ask her to come over," she said, refer-
ring to their longtime neighbor who had always offered
to help if there was an emergency. "Or are you feeling
well enough to walk over there yourself? You know
she's good about letting you stay at her house until one
of us gets there."

"I'm not a kid anymore and I have my inhaler. Can't
you come get me before you head for the hospital?
Dani's a pain, but she's my family, too."

"First let me find out how things are going. I'll call
you as soon as I see Dani."

As she disconnected, she felt Dylan's arms come
around her.

"I couldn't help hearing something was wrong.
What's happened?"

Turning in his arms so she could hold him, too, she
blurted, "My little girl has tried to—" she couldn't
complete the thought "—she's taken something. I've
got to get to her."

"Of course you do. Damn, E.D., I don't know what
to say." Pressing a kiss to her hair, he forced her to arm's
length to study her face. "How can I help? Are you okay
to drive?"

She drew a stabilizing breath. "I don't have a—oh!"
Realizing he was offering to take her, she shook her
head. "That's the last thing we need to risk."

"Then let Chris do it. I'm sure he'd volunteer gladly."

She started heading for the bedroom to dress, her
mind already down the road. "No. Any male outside of
someone from my office would trigger too much attention. I'm sorry about breakfast."

"Forget it. I'll fix you a plate to warm up when you get back. Go."

After dragging on jeans, a white knit sleeveless sweater and briskly brushing her hair into a ponytail, she hurried for the Mercedes. Despite trying to keep her cool, her foot was heavy on the gas pedal and the car kicked up dust as she sped up the driveway. Suddenly, being this far from town had its negative aspects. It would be wise to run through a laser car wash along the way. If Trey happened to see her car with this dust all over the tail end, he would start wondering where she was staying. She'd briefly considered just calling him for an update, but suspected if he did respond, he'd warn her off. No way was she risking that. She needed to see things for herself—even if it meant gambling at possible curiosity about her dirty car.

Fortunately, most people seemed to be sleeping in this morning and traffic was light. In just under a half an hour she was at the hospital. Grateful to find a slot in the first aisle, E.D. parked and ran for the Emergency entrance. Upon giving Dani's name at the reception window, the attendant released the door lock and directed her to the correct location. A good sign, she told herself. Dani wasn't in an operating room, but an observation area.

As she rounded the corner, she spotted Trey several doors down. He was in deep conversation with a petite brunette whom E.D. recognized. Giselle Garza's fashionable wispy hairdo looked a bit damp, either from class or racing to get Dani here, E.D. surmised. The former professional ballerina's hot-pink chiffon skirt over the standard black leotard perfectly outlined her petite dancer's body. What startled E.D. was seeing how Giselle was holding Trey's hand in both of hers.

It was Trey who spotted her. Stiffening, he muttered something to Giselle and freed his hand.

"What are you doing here?" Trey snapped, stepping forward to block her way.

Aware of a passing nurse who was scowling at them, E.D. kept her tone low and as civil as she could stomach. "Dani's my daughter. How is she?"

"Excuse me, I should leave." Giselle stepped forward and gave E.D. a sympathetic look. "I'm so sorry, Mrs. Sessions. I usually lock my desk when I'm holding class, but things were somewhat hectic this morning and I forgot to."

"She took pills from your desk? What were they?"

After shooting Trey a worried look, Giselle whispered, "A mild sedative."

"Why on earth are you keeping sedatives at your dance studio?" E.D. demanded, incredulous.

"You're not the big shot in court prosecuting," Trey ground out. "Give the poor woman a chance to explain, after all she is the one who realized what had happened and got Dani here immediately rather than waiting for an ambulance."

"No, it's all right," Giselle said, her expression miserable. "If Dani were my child, I'd be going insane." She focused her dark, dramatically painted eyes on E.D. "I'd only stopped at the drugstore on my way to the studio. They're over-the-counter and no real harm if taken as prescribed. I have trouble sleeping at times due to chronic pain," she added with a grimace. "What we do for love and all that."

Why hadn't she left them in her car then? E.D. wasn't in the mood to be generous. What if no one had realized what had happened? "How many did she take?"

"About half the bottle, but apparently she came to class on an empty stomach and was soon ill."

"Thank heaven." Pressing a hand to her heart, E.D. tried to think as a lawyer and not a mother; however, the terror and fury driving her emotions wasn't easily controlled. "What I don't understand is why today and at your school? She loves dance and has always said it's the one place where she feels completely alive."

Giselle gestured gracefully. "A few of the girls were rude. On the heels of Dani's…situation, they saw an opportunity to get rid of competition."

"Competition?"

"You aren't aware they're vying for solo spots in the August recital?"

E.D. stifled a groan. She should have remembered that there was always a recital in the summer before school started, but it had apparently slipped her mind. "Yes," she replied, thinking she'd be damned if she gave Trey free ammunition to use against her. "But I wasn't thinking about it at this moment."

Lowering her eyes, Giselle barely succeeded in covering a smile. "Of course. I apologize if I, in any way, suggested you were out of touch. All I wanted to explain is that when Dani burst into tears, I sent her to my office to get some tissues to blow her nose and dry her face. So you see, it's entirely my fault. I should have put one of the senior girls in charge of the rest of the class, directed them to do positions, and gone with Dani. All I can say in explanation is that she'd seemed in control until then, so mature in handling her...misfortune."

More likely she'd been mortified and locked in humiliation and silence, E.D. thought, hurting for her daughter.

"The important thing is that they're not going to have to pump her stomach and the pills weren't inside her long enough to even damage her stomach lining," Trey said with increased impatience. "So, E.D., you can turn right around and leave because I have everything under control."

She shot him a withering look. There was no missing that he found the ordeal embarrassing, not frightening. "I'm not going anywhere without you at least letting her see me.

"As for you having things under control, this proves you don't. Why she went to class, I don't know. She was nowhere near emotionally ready."

"I told her she should. She can't hide in her room forever."

E.D. felt an icy rage freeze her and she wrapped her arms around her waist. "Of all the hypocrisy—you, who refused to come to any evening event I was involved with because you didn't know anyone?

"She was driven to overreacting, Trey, not because she was pretending to be shy or was too lazy to try and get along with others, but because she was emotionally injured. Maybe she needs to succeed before you take her seriously?"

Before Trey could respond, Giselle touched E.D.'s hand. "I should go. You need privacy. I was just waiting to make sure the news was positive. Again, I am so sorry. Please know that I will have a stern talk with the rest of the class. Dani is a beautiful girl and a dancer with great promise. I would hate to think this might keep her from continuing her training."

"That will be Dani's decision," E.D. said with cool politeness.

Moistening her lips, Giselle glanced at Trey and then left.

E.D. turned her back on the departing woman and glared at her estranged husband. "I'm going in there to see her," she said, nodding to the nearest door to where they stood. "But I just want you to know you made another mistake by leaving Mac alone at the house."

"He's fine! I talked to him ten minutes before you got here. He went next door."

"Because I told him to. He was getting anxious and gasping for breath when he called me. She's his flesh and blood and he's a child!"

Shoving his hands into his Dockers, Trey jutted his chin stubbornly. "You've got ten seconds to leave or I'm calling security."

"Go to hell, Trey."

Brushing by him, she went into the room where she found Danielle curled in a fetal position in the narrow bed, her back to the door. Her long blond hair was still in its single braid and fastened in a bun at her nape, but tendrils were working free and were plastered to her forehead and cheek.

As E.D. circled the bed, she whispered, "Dani?"

The girl opened her eyes and whimpered, "Mom."

Relieved when she reached out for her, E.D. settled on the edge of the bed and took her daughter into her arms. "My poor sweetie. You scared me to death."

"My throat hurts," she rasped.

Stroking the teen's slender back, she sighed. "I'll bet it does. I'll tell your father to go get you some Popsicles once he gets you home to your own bed. That should relieve the rawness a bit."

"Thanks." Dani hid her face in E.D.'s shoulder. "I wish I hadn't gone to class. I didn't want to go, but Ms. Garza called and talked Daddy into making me go, even though I told her that I wasn't feeling well."

Giselle? So much for Trey taking credit for what he saw as intelligent reasoning. And shame on that woman for putting her need for customers ahead of a young girl's vulnerable self-esteem, E.D. fumed; as for Trey and this latest lie—

As Dani began to weep softly, E.D. rocked her and stroked her hair. As relieved and overjoyed as she was that her daughter wasn't being hostile to her, she couldn't get over Trey's conduct. But no way could she berate her estranged husband to his daughter.

"He meant well, Dani. He was concerned that you'd get depressed to the point where you would quit, and next drop out of school. Now, I'm not excusing that, but you know he's home all day and doesn't remember or see how tough kids can be on kids. He doesn't witness what I see in my work."

"Then tell him, Mom, because you're right, I'm never going back to school, either. Lindsay and her bunch will have it all over the campus that I've been an idiot again."

At least she was acknowledging that her latest decision had also been a poor one. "There's only ten more days of school," E.D. crooned. "And with your—"

Dani flung herself back onto the bed and resumed her tight fetal position. "I said I *can't*."

Although E.D. knew better than allow herself to be played this way, it felt good to be needed by her independent and often headstrong child. "Let me finish. I was about to say that your grades have been excellent. Under the circumstances, I'll bet we can arrange something with your teachers for you to finish the year at home."

"Promise?"

In the end, E.D.'s common sense and professional shrewdness prevailed. "One gesture of faith deserves another. Will you promise me that you won't do anything like this again? There's always another choice," she said gently but dead serious. "Always."

Someone cleared his throat behind her. Glancing over her shoulder, she saw a security guard in the doorway. Behind him was a nurse peering around his undernourished frame. Kissing Dani's warm forehead, E.D. whispered, "I have to go."

"No! Please stay." Dani sat up again to clutch her tight.

"There's a restraining order, dear. You've heard me speak of them often enough."

With that Dani burst into a new flood of tears.

Her heart breaking, E.D. eased herself out of her daughter's hold. "There's no need for that. I love you and I'll be in touch and see you very soon."

"Leave my mother alone!" Dani cried toward the door. "Daddy, stop *doing* this."

As Dani buried her face in her drawn-up knees, E.D. exhaled, touched her hair, and went to deal with what was coming next.

"Can we step away from the door?" she asked the uniformed man politely. "As you can see the last thing my daughter needs is any more emotional upheaval."

Young but taking his job seriously, the guard asked, "Ma'am, is it true there's a restraining order forbidding you from being anywhere near her?"

Ignoring Trey, E.D. inclined her head. "My husband and I are in the process of divorcing and he's chosen that strategy."

"But disobeying the law means—"

"I'm Deputy D.A. E. D. Martel," she said looking him in the eye. "I know the law. However, Officer, having learned my daughter had experienced what I was told was a life-threatening emergency, a piece of paper obtained through dishonest means doesn't hold much threat to me. If this had happened to your child, what would you do?"

Blushing, the guard replied, "I don't have any kids yet, ma'am. Heck, I'm not even married." Scowling at the nurse who couldn't repress a titter as she squeezed by them to go to Dani, he continued, "Um…the thing is this isn't about me, and…the law is the law."

Where was a pragmatist when she needed one? "Indeed, Officer, and assured that my daughter is at least physically stable—" she cast Trey a you-haven't-heard-the-end-of-this look "—I'm about to take my leave. Will that be adequate for you…Officer Marsh?" she said reading his name plate.

Looking hopeful, the rent-a-cop asked Trey, "Sir? Would that be acceptable with you?"

Trey joined them, but his gaze never rose above E.D.'s breasts. "All right. My daughter has been through enough trauma for one day."

E.D. clenched her keys so tightly that she was certain the moisture she felt was blood. "I promised Dani that I'd ask you to get her some Popsicles after you get her home. She'll need the coolness to relieve the rawness in her throat. If you don't believe me ask this nurse or her doctor. I'll see you at our Tuesday attorneys' meeting."

When E.D. returned to the ranch, she was somewhat calmer, but only because Dani wasn't in any immediate danger. She shouldn't have been surprised to find Dylan's SUV still parked at the cabin. He was, however, nowhere to be seen. Guessing he was over with Chris, she went inside, dropped her bag and keys onto the couch, and collapsed onto a kitchen chair. Her elbows on the table, she moaned and buried her face in her hands. On the way home, she'd phoned Mac and he had been as vocal about needing her as Dani was.

She didn't hear Dylan enter and started when she felt

his hand on her shoulder. Rising, she went into his arms and sighed with relief as he enfolded her close. "Thank you. This is exactly what I needed."

"Are you all right?"

"Yes—and so is Dani, thank heaven." She gave him an abbreviated version of what had occurred.

"Considering how bad things could have gone, that's a relief," Dylan said, continuing to stroke her back.

"Sure, but the fact that she tried to hurt herself cuts me to shreds. It's such a clear cry for help, but the where and how has only added to her humiliation."

"You'll get her help."

He said that with such matter-of-fact confidence that E.D. couldn't help smiling. "Yes, I will."

Releasing her only to frame her face with his hands, he searched her face. "What about Mac?"

"Lonely. Upset. Schooldays aren't too bad because there's homework, but Saturdays are when I take the kids somewhere special, one week him, the next Dani. It's a quality-time thing."

"Does Trey go along?"

Wanting to kiss him for his obvious jealousy, she said, "Let me rephrase—it's a mother-daughter-son quality-time thing. Trey has opportunities all week."

"Bring Mac here."

Her heart clenching, E.D. closed her eyes. "It's a lovely thought. But Trey wouldn't hesitate triggering an Amber Alert. Enough said." Sighing, she touched her cheek. "I need to get to work. I've barely glanced at the witness list for this next case, haven't begun to develop my questions, my strategy…"

Folding his arms over his chest, Dylan listened patiently. "You must be starving. Go work and I'll make you your own omelet. I was hungrier than I thought and ate what I'd meant to save for you."

After a brief chuckle, E.D. sighed. "Too much trouble. Besides, after dealing with Trey, I've lost my appetite."

"I'd like to hear about what happened if you need or want to talk."

"You're wonderful because I know you mean it, but I can't let myself waste another minute on him, and I don't want to discuss him here. Not now. Not after what we've shared. Don't you have things you need to—"

Dylan touched a finger to her lips. "Your answer was perfect. Thank you, darling." He exchanged his finger for a gentle kiss. "The rest I can wait for as long as you need me to."

"What's pressing on your schedule?" she forced herself to ask when all she wanted to do was feel his heart beating against hers.

"I have some campaign material I have to review and okay and a couple of phone conferences."

"The house will feel empty without you."

"Good. You sure I can't make you a BLT before I go?"

"You're too much. Stop."

"Can't. I have an ulterior motive," he said, drawing her completely against his body. "I want to ruin you for any other man who hears that you're going to be free soon."

"You did that a long time ago."

His eyes smoldering blue heat, he murmured, "God, how am I supposed to walk out of here after hearing that?"

To keep him from saying more, E.D. quickly pressed her lips to his, only to find him ready to turn the kiss into a breathtaking moment of intimacy. As it continued, her body tingled, his grew hot and hard. Only when she arched her hips into his did he tear his mouth from hers and, groaning, bury his face against her neck. "I have to go."

"I know."

Raising his head, Dylan's gaze grew sober. "I doubt I can make it back here tonight, but I'd like to call if I won't be disturbing you."

"With luck I'll be in bed hugging your pillow and breathing in your scent."

"Now you've done it." As he approached her, she backed away, until she was backed against the front door. There he flattened one hand against the door and used his other to cup the side of her face. "Five minutes," he entreated. "I can speed on my way back to town."

"I need you alive so we can make that twenty minutes on your next trip."

"Ah, Eva Danielle…I love your idea of rain checks."

Chapter Eleven

"That was entirely inappropriate."

E.D. could care less what Trey's attorney, Jerry Stoddard, said of her testimony or her opinion of her estranged husband. They had been sitting across the table from each other for over an hour and she was as fed up with this anemic upstart in his threadbare polyester suit and rude manners as she was with his client. Where Trey had found him, E.D. didn't want to know, but they suited each other—both acted sullen in an intellectually superior way, with the posture of high-school sophomores.

"Mr. Stoddard," E.D. enunciated, her gaze drilling, "I'll wager your client hasn't even informed you that our daughter was in Emergency over the weekend due to his idea of good parental judgment. I'd think twice before insulting me with your one-sided perspective on my maternal neglect. I doubt any litigator would dare try the same tactics on a male breadwinner of a family working seventy-hour weeks." There, she thought as the slouching man sat up. She enjoyed the look of resentment Stoddard shot Trey. The attorney would never grasp the disappointment and stigma of failure she was experiencing from all of this, but regardless today marked a turning point in Trey's assault on her character. It was about time this suburban ambulance chaser got a full dose of what a liar and sneak his client was.

"Counselor." Alyx tapped her pen on her notebook, until she got Milquetoast Man's attention. "If you agreed to this meeting under false pretenses and don't wish to make serious progress on dissolving this union amicably as my client and I are willing to do, I suggest we adjourn and discuss future dates."

Trey started. "I can't drag this out." As everyone's eyes locked on him, he lowered his gaze to the blank pad and pencil before him, and he abruptly began rolling the pencil back and forth. "I mean I need—I want to get this over with, too. For the kids' sake," he added.

Those last words were such a clear afterthought that Alyx's tongue worked her cheek. "Admirable, Mr. Sessions." She slipped on reading glasses that matched her mahogany hair and flipped several pages in her appointment book. "For a moment there I thought we were interfering with a pressing book deadline." She barely let that dart set in before flipping another page or two, then pointed a manicured nail to a Tuesday in July. "How's the third Tuesday in July? I can make you my first appointment if you can get here by eight-thirty."

"That's two months away," Trey all but croaked. "That's unb—impossible."

At first, E.D. automatically heard *unacceptable*, but her mind corrected her selective hearing and she realized he had, indeed, meant *unbearable*. Either he was a worse writer than she imagined, or had merely caught himself in time from making another condescending remark toward her. She glanced at Alyx to see how she had taken this.

"Well, unless you're able to arrange for a sitter one evening, that's the best that I can do," Alyx said with a matter-of-fact shrug.

It was hardly an exaggeration. What Trey and Jerry couldn't see, but E.D. could, was that this was no act; Alyx had a schedule that would rival a Las Vegas wedding chapel.

Either some common sense must have sunk into Jerry's thinking, or else he was a fair student of Texas Hold 'Em poker and recognized when he was beaten. Taking a long sip of the bottled water Alyx had supplied—without pouring it into the glass she'd provided—he set down the bottle and clasped his hands. "Let's just try to move forward now and see how far we can get?"

E.D. didn't hear or see any movement to suggest he kicked Trey under the table, but their body language from the waist up indicated that he had. *Well, I'll be*, she thought, some of her tension easing. It would seem Trey and his attorney both wanted this divorce settlement as soon as possible. It had to be because neither was in a financial position to hold out for a prolonged litigation.

After glancing at her slender diamond encrusted watch, Alyx nodded. "I can give you another few minutes. How about you, E.D.?"

"I'm due in court in an hour."

"Then let's get the most important issue out of the way. I believe that when we do, the rest will begin to fall into place rather quickly." As Jerry double-blinked at her take-control approach, she continued, "Since it's been brought up, this past weekend's troubling incident gives my client cause to challenge Mr. Sessions's sole custodial rights of their children Dani and Mac. But we would forego a formal court contest—and the increased expense—if Mr. Sessions would agree to handle that personally within twenty-four hours."

Clearly seeing leverage pulled from his grasp, Jerry all but writhed in his chair. "Wait a minute, there's no proof beyond a he-said-she-said—the kid wasn't even home when the event occurred and the pills weren't my client's."

Good Lord, E.D. thought, Trey had told Stoddard. That made the attorney's attitude toward her all the more despicable.

About to tell Alyx that she'd happily haul Trey's butt to court, he leaned over and whispered something to Jerry Stoddard. At first the attorney angrily shook his head and E.D. thought she heard the word *lose*. But after another terse whisper from Trey, Stoddard relented.

"Uh…okay. So be it." Pulling out a restaurant paper napkin from his pocket, Trey's attorney wiped his damp mouth. "My client has decided to take this on the chin."

"You'll take care of this today?" Alyx asked, pressing for clear verbal confirmation. "Ms. Martel will be able to see or call her children without threat by this time tomorrow?"

"Provided it's supervised visitation that is pre-arranged. But it comes at a cost," he added, giving E.D. the once-over.

The man made her want to bathe in lye soap and gargle with bleach. But hearing Alyx delicately clear her throat, E.D. bit her tongue.

"And what would that be?" Alyx purred.

The men conferred again. Alyx pretended to check her cell-phone messages, but the notes she scribbled down were precisely what E.D. heard figure-wise from across the table.

Finally, Jerry Stoddard sat forward and announced a monthly support figure. In that instant, E.D. lost whatever goodwill she would have tried to retain toward Trey.

"I can't afford that," she whispered to Alyx.

Ignoring her, Alyx handed two copies of a one-page typed list across the table. "Texas isn't an alimony state and the judge will have to decide whether Mr. Sessions qualifies as a hardship case after he sees Ms. Martel's generous settlement offer. What you have there is our disclosure of joint assets and debt as of the date of sep-aration. The asterisks indicate monies my client is willing to relinquish to Mr. Sessions. As you can see those are the joint interest-bearing checking account, savings account, the stocks they hold jointly and fifty percent of the money-market fund. This should put Mr. Sessions in solvent shape until we hammer out a more reasonable monthly expense sheet, less his equity in their homestead. In return, we expect Mr. Sessions to forego all claim to any part of my client's 401K."

"Like hell!" Trey came alive as though his chair had been plugged into a 220 electrical outlet. "Half of that's mine, too!"

In your dreams, E.D. thought. "Would you mind re-membering that we have a daughter about to head to college?" she said, barely managing to keep herself in rigid check. "Who's going to pay for that?"

"You have the college-fund accounts," he snapped, not meeting her eyes.

"Which I only established a few years ago once tuition began rising at an inordinate speed. That will help Mac more than it will Dani, but Mac will be going into the sciences, meaning more years in school." His choice of schools would be crucial and costly. They'd been discussing this for years. What had happened? It sounded as though Trey was willing to sacrifice his children's future for…what?

"Maybe Dani will go into show business," Trey blurted out. "Ms. Garza seems to think she's pretty talented. Hey, she could end up supporting us!"

E.D. stared at him, wondering how she could have blocked so much about him for so long. Her revulsion had her almost running from the room.

"Well, just in case Dani decides to follow in her

mother's footsteps," Alyx drawled, "I suggest we leave the division of property as is listed."

Trey mulled this over a moment. "You wouldn't contest me living in the house?"

"It's where our children will feel most stable for the time being."

"Where are you going to live?"

Now he cares? "I'll have to figure that out."

He narrowed his eyes. "Oh, I get it. The big man's finally giving you the—" He pantomimed a backside pat. "Our house is going to be a shack compared to what you'll be living in once you step up to that position."

E.D. rose and, unable to quite keep her voice steady, said to Alyx, "If I don't leave now, I'll be late for court. You'll have to excuse me."

"Wait for me outside," Alyx directed. "I'll only be a second."

Without giving either man another look, E.D. exited the meeting room. To keep herself from popping an antacid, she checked her messages. There was only one—it was from her assistant, Bruce, nervously informing her that they were already at the courthouse.

Not a word from Dylan. She knew he was probably in court himself, but she hadn't seen him since Saturday and despite several phone conversations since, hearing his voice would have helped considerably right now.

The conference door opened and Alyx came out in a rustle of purple silk followed by a whispery scent of exotic spices and ylang-ylang.

"Obnoxious boors. I swear, E.D., I should charge you double for having married such an—"

"Please don't say it. I'm not feeling particularly brilliant at the moment as it is."

Alyx sighed and walked her to the door with an arm around her shoulder. "Sorry. Just hear me on this, okay? When you talk to the kids, fish for any information you can get on what his schedule is like, how often he leaves the house, who calls, and things like that, okay?"

She couldn't care less what Trey did with his time, but that was obviously not the point. "He sounds like he needs money, doesn't he?"

"Yes. Have you ever known him to have a gambling problem? A drinking or drug problem?"

"No. I would leave for work—he'd be asleep. I would return—he'd either be watching TV or still in his office." Playing computer games, she suspected, from a few comments Mac had made in past months.

At the door Alyx touched her arm. "Don't get upset, but the man I hired? E.D... I think he's come upon something."

Unable to help herself, E.D. gasped and stared at her. "What?"

"I should know more soon. Be patient."

"After saying *that?*"

"Give me another week or two." Alyx glanced over her shoulder at the closed door. "E.D., it's my job to look out for your best interests. Don't hate the messenger, hate the jerk who's turned your life inside out."

E.D. had used versions of that line herself; she would never have believed it would be said to her. How smug she'd been to assume she would never find herself in such dire straits.

"I guess he could be gambling online," she murmured. "He can't be doing drugs. I would know…or at least the kids would see something in his behavior." Reaching for the doorknob, she paused. "Have you heard from Jonas Hunter? Is this information from him?"

Alyx took control of the knob and opened the door for her. "Jonas is back in Washington, D.C."

"Oh. Then he wasn't able to help?"

"On the contrary. The photographer's site has been irreparably infected."

"It has?"

"That's my understanding."

For a moment E.D. was cheered. Then her elation waned. "The damage is still done. People have already downloaded Dani's photos. Some are bound to put them on other sites. And what about the negatives for those photos?"

"This situation will never be perfectly resolved, E.D. We don't live in that kind of world anymore, you know that. But things will get better in time. You and Dani both will just have to take comfort in that it could have been a lot worse."

That was true. "So will the FBI go after the guy, this photographer?"

"He's on a list. Jonas told you enough to know they work off a very long list, and it doesn't help that this worm has skipped town for the moment."

That wasn't reassuring news. It might be weeks or even years before he was captured, if ever. How many other young lives would he compromise by then? Repressing a shiver, she focused on Dylan's friend. "I liked Jonas. Did you?"

"He seems adept at his work."

"I mean as a man. He was attracted to you."

With a droll look, Alyx urged her through the doorway. "You've got court, and I have to get back in there and arrange for another meeting."

"Please tell me that July date isn't etched in stone?"

"I know you want this over with as soon as possible. I had a postponement on another case just this morning. We can try for it. A week from Thursday, 2:00 p.m.? I'll call you if it's a go with them. One more thing," she added.

E.D. glanced over her shoulder.

"Err on the side of caution if you're seeing the judge. Be discreet."

E.D. didn't pretend to deny any involvement. "Trey can't afford a private investigator."

"He can now."

"But I've given him no cause."

"Go look in a mirror and assume that Jerry isn't as stupid as he looks."

"Excuse me?" Still reeling from Alyx's parting advice, E.D. thought she'd misunderstood Bruce Littner's mumbled expletive.

"Reverend Leroy Betts isn't on the witness list," he repeated, leaning over and pointing to her copy of the papers they'd given the judge and the defense team.

E.D. shook her head. "He has to be. He was in my notes."

"Well, somehow between those notes and the actual list the clerk typed, he's not there." Bruce sighed. "I should have caught that. It's my job to proof the paperwork."

Feeling as though she were sliding back down into the black hole she'd only begun to climb out of, E.D. stared at the list and knew they were in deep trouble. "It's everyone's job, including mine." Reverend Betts was vital to their strategy because he was the one person who had proof that the defense's two witnesses were flagrant liars and the minister's testimony could confirm the prosecution's time line that put the accused at the murder scene. A respected minister—of all people to risk losing on the stand!

"Do you think the judge will let you add him on? Opening statements have only just been completed. It's not like we've started the interrogatory phase."

"Maybe. Possibly not." Either way it would be announcing to the court and defense that she wasn't up to par professionally and even if the press didn't get wind of that, Emmett would. God, she didn't need this. "All I can do is try."

"Let me."

Respecting Bruce more than ever, E.D. squeezed his arm. "You're not falling on a sword for my lack of concentration." Slowly rising, she began deferentially, "Your honor, may I approach the bench?"

Some five hours later, E.D. entered the D.A.'s offices and didn't get halfway down the hall before a flustered paralegal emerged from Emmett's office. "Oh, Ms. Martel…thank goodness! He's looking for you."

E.D. had no doubt that he was. "I've only just returned from court. Thanks, Torrie."

Hoping that she was wrong in her assumption of what Emmett wanted, she managed a warm smile for the young woman and knocked on the door. But the way the day had gone, she doubted she would be that lucky.

"Enter."

She winced, recognizing that razor-sharp tone. Opening the door, she saw Emmett sitting behind his massive desk in shirtsleeves and vest, his silver hair impeccably brushed, and his distinguished face a mask of cold displeasure.

After removing his wire glasses, he tossed them onto the brief he'd been reading. "If you think you'll make points for showing up now to take your medicine instead of waiting for the morning meeting, you're wrong," he said without preamble.

How he'd found out, she didn't know. More than likely Judge Rosen himself had called him. "I've only arrived from court, sir," she repeated quietly.

"I'm not surprised you were stuck there all day, considering how ill-prepared you are for your case."

E.D.'s grip on her briefcase tightened, but she remained silent. She knew to try to defend herself at this point would be a critical misstep.

"This is an untenable situation," Emmett railed on. "Why did it happen? A first-year paralegal doesn't make that kind of mistake. He's a man of the cloth. The fact that you didn't see his title should have leapt off the page at you."

"That's true, sir."

"A minister of such unimpeachable reputation, you could have had no list whatsoever, only him, and you would have won the case."

When she remained silent, Emmett lifted an eyebrow. "No excuse?"

"No, sir."

But he was clearly demanding one so that he could purge his anger by tearing it and her to shreds. "Excuse my sloppy semantics—an explanation then, if you please. There has to be one. E. D. Martel doesn't lose a case on the first day of hearing testimony."

An explanation, she thought, hoping she could make it to the ladies' lounge before becoming physically ill. What could she say—an overloaded docket? Virtually no life and little rest? Or actually, she amended as Dylan's face flashed before her eyes, finally a life and a good deal of preoccupation regarding that possibility. Dear heaven, she'd as soon grab the sterling-and-crystal letter opener on her boss' desk and slit her throat than to confess that.

E.D. swallowed. "I wouldn't waste your time, sir."

"I suppose I should be grateful for that much." Looking anything but mollified, Emmett demanded, "What's your strategy to save the case?"

Emmett might not be ready to fire her, but he wasn't about to cut her any slack. She thought of the options she'd already considered and picked the one she thought had the best potential for satisfying him. "The good reverend's secretary *is* on the list. She won't know until she's on the stand that he can't be called because the judge wouldn't allow it this late. I plan to revise my questions to where she will have to inform the court that he does have knowledge of the whereabouts of the accused."

"Which can never be confirmed by him. You must know defense will object and the judge could sustain. It's too transparent."

Yes, it was. But at the moment it was the best she could do.

"Do not let this case be your undoing," Emmett warned softly. "Do I make myself clear, E.D.?"

"Crystal clear, sir."

Chapter Twelve

"Thank you for giving me another opportunity."

It was Saturday night and the ballroom of the hotel was filling fast for one of Austin's more prestigious charity events. With his attention on the entrance to the ballroom, Dylan didn't initially grasp that the appreciative comment had been directed at him.

"Judge?"

"Pardon? Kent Ward—how the heck are you?" Dylan extended his hand to the young man who had once clerked for him. Things had been rocky at first, but despite initial misgivings—and some stern late-night lectures—the rebel from rural Texas had championed his demons. Dylan had been able to send him on to the next stage of his career confident he would become a thoughtful and fair member of the bar. "Cleaning up well these days."

"Thank you, sir." Kent squirmed a little, and tugged at his collar, his beefy frame the type more often seen in denim work clothes. "The tux is still a rental. I figure I'm a ways from owning one of my own, but you may be proud to know I'm midway through a solid five-year plan."

"I am. Congratulations," Dylan added, understanding how far his former protégée had come. "Childs, Eubanks and Fairchild is an outstanding firm. You made a good move going with them."

"Thank you, sir."

The younger man's flushed countenance and beaming smile had Dylan feeling like an old law professor. "You'll have a fine career, Kent. Now try to remember to enjoy the journey."

"I will." The younger man nodded, then grew serious. "Sir—you were the best mentor a train wreck like me could ask for, and I sure don't know how I got so lucky. The only reason I put on this monkey suit was because I hoped to run into you and say that—and also how proud I am to hear you're aiming for the top judicial vacancy. You'll get my vote."

Touched, Dylan shook hands with the state's newest lawyer. "Thank you. We'll see if you hold to that opinion of me down the road when you bring me a case."

Blushing again, Kent Ward demurred. "I doubt that will ever happen. Heck, you'll recuse yourself at the first sight of my name on your docket."

"You've got that right."

Kent grew somber. "But it would be a privilege to beat you to it, sir."

Feeling a lump in his throat, Dylan pretended to give him a squinty-eyed study. "You're not about to ask me for a West Point letter of recommendation for a kid brother or sister, are you?"

The equally broad-shouldered man chuckled. "As bright as she is, it could happen, sir."

As he moved on, Dylan wished him luck again, then his smile deepened as his gaze fell on the newest arrival in the ballroom. It had been a full week since he'd last seen E.D. A long week of missed phone calls, abbreviated phone calls, but also a couple of downright erotic conversations with her in the deep of the night. From the way his insides clenched and his heart tripped over itself as he watched her pause to chat with an elderly couple, he knew that regardless of risk, one way or another, he would have her in his arms tonight.

She looked like a goddess stepped down from Olympus in her off-the-shoulder, claret-red gown and her hair shimmering silver and gold in a regal chignon. Heads turned as she made her way through the crowd, next pausing to greet this year's chairman of the ball, then assorted city and state powerbrokers. Not once did he see or sense a hint of the woman whose private life was in crisis. She had too much class and dignity to stumble before this crowd.

Dylan did his own PR work, but all the while he kept one eye on her like the jealous lover that he was. It took him almost fifteen minutes before he managed to achieve a face-to-face meeting. When it finally occurred, it was thanks to fellow judge Roger Chambers.

"Dylan, you know E.D.," the jovial senior judge said, taking hold of his arm. "Come help convince her to partner me at my weekly bridge club while Alice is in Europe. You can vouch that I'm as trustworthy as a monk."

"Hmm." Dylan pretended to consider that request, then leaned toward E.D. and with a conspiratorial air whispered, "Do yourself a favor and run like hell. The only reason Alice risks those trips is because he knows she has cameras hidden all over the house."

As Roger threw back his head to laugh with gusto, Dylan accepted E.D.'s offered hand, finding it unusually cool for late May. That confirmed what this close vantage point already told him: she was functioning on sheer determination alone. "Good to see you, E.D."

"And you, Judge."

Although her makeup was flawless, and her skin exquisite, Dylan thought she looked too fragile. He knew she'd endured another hellish week and could tell she'd lost another pound or two that she could ill afford. But it was the wounded look shadowing her lovely brown eyes that troubled him the most, and intensified the yearning in his heart to hold and comfort her. "Let me offer a polite excuse to escape this old mauler," he drawled, smoothly tucking her hand in the crook of his elbow. "Come dance with me. Back in my schooldays I was voted least likely to inflict injury on the dance floor."

"Well, with these heels, I'm not sure you can live up to that reputation, or that I won't do some damage myself," she replied, glancing down at her sexy slides, "but if it means staying in Alice's good graces, lead on. Bye, Judge Chambers."

With a victorious wink at his old friend, Dylan cut a circuitous path to the dance floor. Just as he and E.D. reached it, the orchestra on the stage began playing "As Time Goes By" from *Casablanca.* The lights were dim on this side of the room, and as he drew her into his arms, he noted that her eyes shimmered as much as her pearl-and-diamond teardrop earrings.

"My God, you are especially beautiful tonight," he murmured.

"Dylan…someone will hear."

"I don't care."

"Start. This is madness."

"So is having to keep my distance. I've missed you." Proof of that was how effortlessly his body aligned itself to hers.

"Me, too," she said, her breath warming his shoulder.

"Say that again against my neck. Those are serious high heels all right. You're almost tall enough to give me a love bite."

She choked on a laugh. "You're being incorrigible."

"Wait, I'll turn you around. While everyone thinks you're admiring the brocade wallpaper, you can do it."

"I will not."

"One little bite with those pretty teeth, that's all I'm asking for."

"*Stop*. You're attracting too much attention as it is."

Dylan sighed. "Lady Godiva attracted less attention than you do in that dress, and you're complaining about me?"

"I suppose it was a mistake, but I needed the morale boost. I'm running low on courage tonight."

"My poor darling. I wish there was more that I could do. You do have me worried. Why don't we head toward the buffet? When was the last time you swallowed more than air?"

"The mere thought of food makes me nauseous. Have you seen Emmett?"

Dylan frowned at the concern in her voice. "Earlier. He was safely self-possessed, making the rounds, schmoozing the right people, looking for new backers."

"I need to avoid him if possible."

"What's he done now?" She'd told him about the witness error and Emmett's reaction. As bad as the blunder was for a veteran, Dylan thought E.D.'s track record and personal issues made her deserving of a little understanding.

"Nothing. It's Dani. I just don't have the energy or brain cells left to spar with him." E.D. made an unintelligible sound. "Dylan, she isn't doing her schoolwork. I was reduced to begging before her school's principal agreed to let her do her assignments from the house, and does the girl cooperate? No. She sleeps all day—when she isn't sobbing or launching into hysterics over something in her e-mail in-box. The homebound teacher has about given up on her and says if I can't get her motivated, she'll get an incomplete. That means not only does she not graduate with the class, she'll have to go to summer school if she wants to start college in the fall."

Something didn't add up for Dylan. "What's Daddy Dearest been doing while all of this has been going on?"

"I have no idea. The last two times the homebound teacher stopped by, he wasn't there. With my luck he's busy conspiring something else with his attorney. I do wish Alyx's PI would surface with some information. The last time I spoke with her, she was irked that he was giving another client priority."

"I hate to say it, but it sounds as though Dani may need a few sessions with a therapist," Dylan said.

"I agree and have broached the subject. The problem is getting her there. She's no more amenable to that than she is to school."

"At least Trey is living up to his promise to let you see her and Mac."

"Barely...and believe me, his condescension almost kills any joy I get from those few minutes of contact here and there."

Dylan couldn't help but tighten his arms around her. "I swear, if I knew it wouldn't hurt your case, I'd go knock some sense into that useless piece of—"

"My hero," E.D. said tenderly.

"I want to be." Although his voice was gruff from pent-up emotion, Dylan needed to get the words out. "I want to be everything to you."

"Oh, God...you can't say things like that."

"Why not? It's true."

"Because...you make me want, no, *yearn* for things that are impossible right now. Maybe forever."

"Like hell they are." Keeping a firm hold of one of her hands, Dylan led her off the dance floor.

"What are you doing?" she whispered.

He ignored her until they were in the lobby. "Escorting you to the ladies' lounge. You hide out there for a minute, then head for the valet station and get your car. I'm going there now and will wait for you down the road."

"I've only just arrived."

"You've been here at least thirty minutes. Plenty of people make an appearance and then leave."

"No one is going to be fooled."

Dylan shoved his hands in his pockets to keep from taking hold of her shoulders and doing what he most wanted to do. "You've got five seconds to give me your most professional smile and say 'Good night, Judge,'" he warned under his breath, "or I'm going to kiss you until you'll need the wall to help you stand."

As twin spots of color appeared on her cheeks, she clutched her tiny beaded evening bag to her heart. She didn't smile, but she did manage to say, "Thank you for the dance, Judge."

Exhaling, Dylan bowed his head. "It was a pleasure, E.D. I hope you're feeling better soon."

E.D. spun on her heel and headed for the ladies' room. Her insides were quaking and her mood was incendiary.

How dare he! How could he?

But the tears that blurred her vision were from mental and emotional fatigue as much as indignation at being practically blackmailed by Dylan. Blinking them away, she didn't realize she was headed straight into someone until he caught her by the shoulders and steadied her.

"Oh, I'm sorry, I—" E.D. glanced down to shift her

foot back into her right shoe. When she looked up again, her heart lurched.

The person who had come to her rescue was none other than Emmett Garner and, if possible, he looked angrier than he had the other day in his office.

"Have you lost your mind?" he ground out.

E.D. couldn't have been more horrified if she'd come face-to-face with a spitting cobra. "Excuse me, sir. I'm afraid I'm a little under the weather and didn't see where I was going."

"Do not attempt to claim contamination from peroxide for your lack of sensibility, Ms. Martel. I witnessed you and Judge Justiss on the dance floor, as well as that little scene a moment ago."

Honestly sick to her stomach, E.D. could barely meet his furious gaze. "You'll have to excuse me. I really need—"

As she tried to step around him, Emmett gripped her arm to stop her. "Listen, my girl, at another time and with different circumstances, I'd give my wholehearted blessing, but not now. Do I make myself clear? *Not now*."

He released her and strode away, leaving a reeling E.D. to glance around to see how many people had witnessed that humiliation. To her relief, the only ones in the area were a couple heading for the elevators and apparently oblivious to what had occurred. Thinking *small gifts,* E.D. decided to forego the lounge farce and headed for the valet window herself.

Dylan finally caught up to E.D.'s Mercedes a few miles away from his ranch. Early on, he'd briefly extinguished his headlights to reassure her of who was behind her, then had followed her the rest of the way. *Chased* was the accurate description. He would never have guessed her a speeder and knew better than to conclude it was due to any uncontrollable desire to be in his arms—to murder maybe. That left one other possibility....

At the cabin, he burst from his SUV as fast as she did her sedan. "What was that all about?"

"Don't start. Not one word." E.D. pointed to the house. "I just want to change, get my things, and leave."

As she fumbled with her purse for her key, Dylan dealt with the shock of what she'd announced; nevertheless, he beat her to the task, reasoning that once inside they could talk. He could apologize and explain his motivation had simply been to get her out of that hotel as soon as possible. But once he had the door open, things didn't improve.

E.D. tiptoed inside like a geisha in her precarious heels and narrow skirt, and, while he locked up, she slipped off her shoes.

"Don't do that," she said. "I mean it—I'm leaving."

Turning to face her, he saw she was watching him and her expression said she was serious. No, he thought again, this was going to be worse than he'd anticipated.

"Okay," he began, "let me start by apologizing and say that I was just worried and selfish tonight, and wanted you out of there and here with me."

"Well, do you know who witnessed the whole thing and cornered me after you left?" E.D. tugged off her earrings and dropped them into her bag. "My boss.

Exactly what I warned you about. Exactly the person I needed to avoid."

Dylan grimaced. "I'm sorry. Damn. What did he say?"

"What do you think? I'm the walking plague and I should stay away from you. I'm a danger to your career and, should I succeed in hurting your election, his chances would possibly be compromised, as well. Ergo, what a good idea it would be to get out of your life." With that she grabbed a handful of her narrow skirt and headed down the hall.

Silently cursing the meddling prosecutor, Dylan followed her. His heart pounded against his sternum. Get out of his life? Never!

"I'm sorry," he told her as he followed her into the dimly lit bedroom. "Can we discuss this?"

"There's nothing to discuss." She dropped her things onto the chair beside the closet and reached behind herself for the dress's zipper. "He's right and I'm getting out before I hurt you and lose my job."

"Where are you going to go?"

"If I tell you, doesn't that defeat the purpose?"

"A hotel. That's crazy. At this hour?"

"Blasted zipper," she muttered tugging.

"Hold it." Dylan crossed to her. "Some of the material is caught in there. Let me help."

He could tell by the way she stiffened that she didn't want him anywhere near her, never mind touching her. Carefully easing the zipper back up until he could get it free again, he then drew it down completely.

"Thank you," she said quietly. "Now would you mind leaving?"

"Yes, I do. We're still talking."

"I need to change."

"Stay the night, E.D. There's no way I'm going to let you drive back into town at this hour, and if you try, I'll only follow you, which—speaking of defeated purposes—cancels the reason for you to run away from me."

E.D. spun around, holding the bodice to herself to keep it from falling to her ankles. "I'm not running away."

"Running away," he intoned and folded his arms over his chest. "And where's my vote in all of this?"

"He's my boss."

"Stay here," Dylan coaxed.

Opening her mouth to reply, E.D. abruptly exhaled. "Fine. I will. Now please go."

"Promise."

"I don't need to promise, I've given you my word."

"Then do one more thing for me," he murmured, cupping her chin and caressing her lower lip with his thumb. "Let me stay with you."

"That—" She closed her eyes. "You're impossible."

He smiled tenderly. "Sorry. It's habitual where you're concerned."

"Don't joke. You just don't get it."

"I *get* that I need to touch you. Hold you." And he did, slowly sliding his hands up her bare arms to draw her across the few inches that separated them, then lowered his head to brush his lips against hers. When she refused to respond, he coaxed, "Kiss me back, Eva Danielle. I've been aching for you to all week."

"Dylan, you're breaking my heart."

"No, I'm not. I'm offering you mine."

Patient, he waited until, finally, she reached up with her free hand to the back of his head and gave him what he wanted. Relief, joy and desire welled up from his soul; he could only liken it to the first instant of morning sunlight touching his skin. Locking his mouth to hers, he drank in her moan and lifted her into his arms.

She'd scared the hell out of him a moment ago and he needed to feel every inch of her precious body to quell the panic he'd felt. He'd lost her once. It could never happen again.

Trapped by the silk that kept her arms at her sides, E.D. broke the kiss. "Put me down so that I can get out of this straitjacket."

The only reason Dylan did was that he wanted her arms around him, too. The second reason came the instant she stood and let the dress drop to a crimson puddle around her. She looked like a mermaid with her strapless bra and bikini panties, both adorned with seashells in strategic places.

"And I thought that dress was the ultimate provocation," he said with renewed hunger pulling in his belly.

Although she shook her head at his blatant flattery, E.D. stepped over the dress to remove his bow tie, then his jacket. "No one looks like you do in a tuxedo," she told him. "Not even Emmett, whom I have to admit is about as distinguished as they come even in a business suit."

Dylan responded with a low growl as he removed his cufflinks. "Can we not mention him anymore tonight?"

E.D. deftly dealt with the shirt's buttons while he

dropped the gold cufflinks onto the chair beside her things. Smiling, she slid off his shirt, then nuzzled the mat of hair covering his chest. "Even when it ends up complimenting you?"

As he reached for the black cummerbund at his waist, he gave her a lecherous look. "You want to compliment me, lie down."

Although she chuckled softly, E.D. instead turned away to draw the pins out of her hair and place them on the chest of drawers across the room.

Dylan drank in her beauty as he continued to strip. He knew he would never tire of watching her perform those simple tasks because her every movement was marked by grace. As her hair tumbled down her back like a gold-and-silver curtain, he went to her and released the hooks on her bra, then slid his hands around her to cup her breasts. Whether it was the cool air-conditioning or his touch, her nipples were already taut. He promised himself that he would make them harder with his tongue and mouth.

"Come here," he murmured.

To his delight, as he coaxed her to face him, she sprang into his arms and wrapped her legs around him. Murmuring his appreciation, he carried her to the bed and lowered them both onto the turned-down sheets. As his hardness pressed against the sole seashell blocking him from ecstasy, Dylan locked his mouth to hers for a deep, probing kiss.

E.D. whimpered and gripped his buttocks, holding him closer as she writhed beneath him. The longer he kissed her, the more she twisted and arched, until with a mew of entreaty, she urged his hands to her panties.

Dylan wanted them off, too, but understood the limits of his endurance. First, he needed to know she was as ready as he was. Slowly easing down her slender length, he bestowed kiss after thorough kiss—to her collarbone, her breasts, then her flat tummy. When he reached the bit of silk covering her hips, he blew softly against the flirty little shell, enjoying her sudden gasp and the way she trembled; then he took hold of the waistband with his teeth and continued sliding downward.

On his return, he gently scored her calf with his teeth, then the inside of her knee and both thighs. When his breath teased the golden curls between her legs, E.D. shied away.

"I don't think I could bear it."

Some note of fear in her voice demanded the question. "How long has it been, my love?"

"Only once." At his sound of disbelief, she turned her head away. "He didn't like to."

Bastard, Dylan thought, and tenderly cupping her slender hips with his hands, he showed her that he adored every inch of her.

She was still gasping and trembling as he rose over and into her. Once he was confident she was moist enough to accept all of him, he thrust himself to the hilt and shuddered with his own pleasure. Linking his fingers with hers, he withdrew, only to repeat the motion, his chest tightening with love and pride as he felt her soft gasp and the beginning of her second orgasm.

"We fight for this...for us," he said against her lips. "Agreed?"

"Yes."

"Nothing, nothing separates us again."

"Dylan..." she begged.

He gave her what she needed, what they both needed, and a second before crushing his mouth to hers, he rasped, "I love you."

Chapter Thirteen

The bliss in opening her eyes was realizing it was Sunday. It turned into heaven when E.D. realized the dream about Dylan wasn't a dream at all; she really was spooned against him, held there by his strong arm across her waist. Closing her eyes, she basked in pleasure. She couldn't remember the last time she'd slept in the nude, let alone felt a man's early morning desire for her stirring between her warm thighs.

"Don't pretend you're asleep," Dylan murmured against her hair.

She smiled. "No. Just appreciating the moment—and not having to jump out of bed and race to court." She stroked the forearm that tucked her closer, loving the obvious masculine traits. "Have you been awake long?"

"Long enough to convince myself you really did stay with me."

Although E.D. still thought leaving would have been the wiser move, she brought his hand to her lips and kissed his knuckles. "I gave you my word."

"Is that the only reason you didn't go?"

"No. My heart refused to listen to my head."

Dylan shifted to kiss her shoulder. "That deserves a back scrub."

"Why don't you go turn on the shower while I detour for a second and turn on the coffee machine?"

He uttered a deep-throated sound of contentment. "Caffeine. You're out to seduce me again."

"Poor man."

Chuckling, he planted a kiss to the back of her head, then rolled over and bounded off the bed and into the bathroom. E.D. took the time to slip on Dylan's tuxedo shirt, which covered her to her thighs. On the way to the kitchen, she paused to use the main restroom before padding barefoot through the quiet house. The morning sun rose on the living-room side, so the kitchen was all soothing shadows that extended outside beyond the covered patio. That was why as she began preparing the machine, the last thing she expected was for one of the shadows to move.

Gasping, she spun around to stare out through the patio doors.

No one was there. A good-sized bird must have flown low on the hunt for a rabbit or gopher, she thought. About to turn back to her measuring, something moved by the kitchen window—something too large to be a bird.

Momentarily clasping her hand over her mouth to keep from crying out, E.D. recovered quickly and started fastening the buttons on Dylan's shirt. She didn't hear any machinery yet, but she suspected Chris was out there about to start mowing before the day's heat set in.

But as she carried the coffeepot to the sink to fill it with water, she changed her mind. Chris was out there, all right, and he was back by the storage building; only instead of rolling out a mower, he was cautiously inspecting the shed, a rifle pointed to the ground in his right hand.

What on earth...? E.D. hurried to the door and unlocked it. "Chris?" she called out. "Is something wrong?"

The moment he turned and spotted her, the exceedingly circumspect cowboy tugged his straw hat lower over his eyes and addressed the patio furniture. "Pardon the disturbance, ma'am. Ah...couldn't help but notice the judge's vehicle out front."

There was no denying the obvious. Besides, she was feeling increasingly disturbed by the way the ranch hand kept searching the area. "Do you need me to get him for you?"

"I'd appreciate it."

In her whole professional career, E.D. had never needed the weapon she was by license and training qualified to carry, but something in Chris's demeanor had her doing a quick mental run-through of its location and the number of bullets in the clip. "Did you see someone around the house?"

"No, ma'am. But ol' Lefty there," he said nodding to the border collie mix canine who sat quietly almost out of E.D.'s line of vision, "he's been unsettled all night, and it wasn't over coyotes."

"I'll get Dylan," she told him.

In the space of a half an hour, the romantic morning turned into something unsettling. Chris reported to Dylan that he was certain someone had been trespassing on the premises last night, and he didn't believe it was the occasional illegals bent on avoiding the highways and detection. Through the other man's recap, Dylan listened patiently, sipping the coffee E.D. had poured for the three of them. He'd quickly pulled on jeans and a light denim shirt, but had yet to fasten more than one snap on the shirt.

"You know I do a spontaneous perimeter check, especially these days," he told his boss as they all sat at the kitchen table. "Well, sometime after you two pulled in last night, someone else turned in front of the gate."

"Did the cameras catch that?"

"No, the angle picks up anyone getting as far as the gate itself. Whoever this was didn't do that. But it looks like he didn't go away, either. I think he eased down the road a ways and came over the barbed-wire fence. Lefty acted up some last night, then settled down. This morning, though, when he came to a section of the fence, he got all antsy again, and followed the trail to here. And there was a bit of material hung on one barb, like a shirt got hung and ripped."

E.D. met Dylan's enigmatic gaze. He had on his

judge's face and there was no point in trying to gauge the depth of his displeasure or his concern as to how serious this news was for them. She knew she would just have to wait until they were alone for that.

It was another few minutes before Chris took his leave. Dylan rose with him and at the door gripped his shoulder and shook his hand.

"I appreciate your thoroughness. Keep a sharp eye, and if anything seems off again, call the sheriff even before you call me. Take no risks, understood?"

"Yes, sir." Picking up his rifle that he'd left leaning against the wall at the door, Chris touched the brim of his hat and nodded to E.D. "Ma'am."

As Dylan closed the door behind him, E.D. rose and carried their mugs to the counter. "Do you want another coffee?" she asked him.

"Please."

His formality triggered a cold something going down her back. As she poured, she asked, "Do you think we were followed back here last night?"

"I didn't see any lights in my rearview mirror. But then someone would have to be pretty fast to keep up because I had my work cut out for me to not lose you."

He was trying to make light out of her question, but his eyes relayed his real, troubled feelings. "Maybe the person already knew how to get here," she said attempting to stop, "and was parked somewhere and waiting."

"It was probably kids playing chicken. It's graduation time and you know every year the news is full of stories of how a couple of them try to outdo each other in the dare-you department."

"Dylan, don't patronize me," she said, bringing him the steaming mug. "You heard Chris. Lefty followed the trail around our vehicles, and then around the house. That's scary."

Dylan promptly set the mug on the counter and drew E.D. into his arms. "Damn it, I know. *I know*. I'm just trying not to upset you any more than you are."

Now she was filled with dread as much as fear. "This isn't about kids, it's about me. You should have let me leave, Dylan. You shouldn't have—"

He silenced her with a kiss that had E.D. rising on tiptoe to get closer to him.

She had dragged on jeans, too, and had exchanged his shirt for a less provocative look, namely last night's bra and a black T-shirt. The extra layers of clothes did nothing to diminish how fiercely Dylan's heart was pounding against hers, and as his kiss staked claim, his strong hands roamed over her back and hips in their own act of possession.

As abruptly as it began, Dylan tore his lips from hers and pressed her face into his shoulder. "God, I'm sorry. Did I hurt you?"

She suspected it would be a few more seconds before she could stand on her own two feet, and her lips were still tingling, but his feelings for her far outweighed that. "I'm all right. I'm better than all right when I'm in your arms— only, Dylan, you have to stop fighting me on this issue."

"Don't say what I think you're going to say."

E.D. leaned back to look at him. "You have to listen. This invasion of your property—things are going from bad to out of control."

"So your conclusion is for me to abandon you? Throw you to the wolves? What?" With a sigh, he folded her more gently against him and rested his cheek against her head. "Forget it, darling."

He was romance incarnate. E.D. had always suspected as much. She already knew he was noble to a fault, and this unyielding determination to protect just made him all the more irresistible; however, somehow she had to protect him from himself. Her conscience would never give her another moment's peace if her problems cost him his future.

"Instead of plotting against me," Dylan said, breaking into her thoughts, "I'd rather hear what I think I already know."

E.D. didn't pretend not to understand. Tilting back her head, she met his searching gaze. While he'd said those three words, she'd only showed him. She thought waiting until this was resolved would somehow provide him with the right to step back if things went badly. Instead, she'd caused him doubt and perhaps even hurt.

"One of my favorite lines in a book was in a romance novel I read as a teenager," she said, reaching up and laying her hand against his dear face. "The heroine tells the hero, 'What I say three times is true,' and then she says, 'I love you, I love you, I love you.'"

Dylan took hold of her hand and pressed a kiss into her palm. "That would work for me."

If she hadn't felt the subtle tremor in his strong body, she would have understood the impact of her words by the gruffness in his voice. With her eyes welling, she whispered, "I love you, I love you…I love you."

"My Eva Danielle."

Their next kiss was about grace and treasuring this precious moment. E.D. didn't know if she had the right to feel so much happiness, but she reached for it, for Dylan, with her heart and soul. *Please*, she prayed, *please let it be all right…and if it can't be, please keep him safe always.*

On Monday evening, E.D. got her answer when she drove to her family residence. She'd called Trey to ask his permission to come over after she left the office. It might be Memorial Day but there was no such break in her office for remembrance of anything but pending litigation. She and Dylan had pondered options regarding Trey on Sunday, and Dylan had been the one to bring the question of their dilemma back to Dani.

"Who signed that permission slip?" he'd said, voicing the ultimate question. "That has to be the key to everything."

As sad as it was, E.D. knew that person had to be Dani. Of course the girl would be too ashamed and afraid to admit she'd forged E.D.'s name, but E.D. needed that confession. Not only did she want Trey to hear so that she could clear her name and reputation, she hoped to get Emmett's support and bring the case to the police in order to have this photographer legally punished.

She'd been relieved when Trey had agreed to the visit. She hadn't told him the real reason she wanted to speak to their daughter; rather, she'd used the call from Dani's homebound teacher. That wasn't a lie because they needed to address that, too. Thankfully, Trey had sounded relieved.

"I hope you do have better luck than me," he'd said. "I'm sick of her whining and her attitude. I swear if Mac turns out to be half as much of a pain when he's her age, I'm going to go stark-raving mad."

It was barely five o'clock when she pulled into the driveway thanks to the lighter traffic downtown. Pre-occupied with how she would approach Dani, E.D. wasn't prepared to see Trey's car in the driveway. She'd hoped he would voluntarily make himself absent. If he was fed up with Dani's behavior, surely he would have concluded any disciplinary discussion would trigger more of the same and want to avoid it?

When she rang the doorbell, he opened the door so quickly, he must have heard her arrival and been wait-ing on the other side. E.D. felt a twinge of apprehen-sion, which grew when she studied his expression.

Trey could do smug too well. With the beginnings of a receding hairline and his chin pressing toward his chest, as he silently stepped back and theatrically motioned for her to enter, his face looked all the rounder and puffy. Wondering if his heightened coloring was due to drinking, she stepped by him, deciding to choose her words carefully.

"It's good of you to let me come by so close to dinner, Trey. I'll try not to be too long and ruin your schedule."

"Mac's having his TV dinner in his room because he's grounded for giving me lip, and your daughter does what she likes when she damned likes it. But before you go upstairs to talk to her, I'd like you to step into my office and see something."

An invitation into the inner sanctum set off additional alarm bells in E.D. She'd never felt physically threatened by him, but had prosecuted enough murderers to know that virtually everyone was capable of anything under the right circumstances. And what if the children weren't home as she'd been led to believe?

Deciding to keep her keys in her hand, with the sharp edge of the ignition key between her thumb and index finger in case she needed to defend herself, she did oblige his second invitation to preceed him, but asked, "All right. What's up?"

"Oh, life in general, me in particular. In fact, things are looking better for me all the time." As he followed her into his office, he closed the door.

E.D. spun around, looking from the door to him. "What's going on, Trey?"

"Why don't you tell me?" he said, crossing his arms over his chest. "After all, in your line of work, you're always telling people that confession is good for the soul."

"Please tell me you haven't been drinking?"

"No, but I do believe I may open a bottle of bubbly to celebrate after you leave."

That was a hopeful sign, wasn't it? He intended her to leave at some point—but did he mean on her own two feet or…? E.D. moistened her lips. "Celebrate what?"

With a tight-lipped smile, Trey gestured toward his desk. "Have a look."

Glancing over there, E.D.'s stomach did a flip-flop.

Several photos were spread across the top of his closed laptop computer. They were all fairly dark and that told her that she didn't need to get closer to know what they were of. She made herself do so anyway to buy herself time and to keep the panic out of her voice.

Circling his desk, she stood above the laptop and gazed down to see the photographer had taken a shot of license plates, vehicles from a distance to show they were parked next to each other, and farther yet to indicate Dylan's cabin. A flash had to have been used, but of course, neither she nor Dylan would have seen the light going off repeatedly because they'd been wholly involved with each other. Chris couldn't have, either, due to the trees that separated the cabins.

"And what is this supposed to mean?" she finally asked with a blank stare.

"Oh, you are as cold out of bed as you are in it," he said, sneering and coming around the other side of the desk. "You must be a pretty good actress to convince your lover otherwise. What's the attraction, sweetie? Are you parting your legs for him hoping his reputation will make it easier for you to move up into your boss's chair?"

E.D. could happily have slapped him for his crudeness; instead she clenched both hands and said coldly, "Thank you for admitting you've been trespassing. I hope you realize that if you care to use those photographs you'll be prosecuted."

"Not me. I didn't take them. They were…a gift that I received only this afternoon."

What?

Trey's gaze hardened. "Just tell me one thing—how long have you been playing me for a fool?"

"I'm not going to dignify that with an answer."

Seeing her chance, she scrambled for the door, yanked it open and began to run for the front door. Unfortunately her high heels were treacherous on the Italian tile floor, and Trey had no trouble catching up with her. Grabbing her arm, he swung her around.

"Not so fast," he snapped. "I have a right to know!"

"We're separated, Trey." E.D. jerked free from his grasp. "You have no rights—not to my business and none to lay a finger on me. If you don't want to face assault charges, keep that in mind."

"You're not the one who's in the position to threaten. I have the evidence that's going to finish getting me everything I want, dear *wife*. What's it worth to you to save your career? Hey, maybe I should ask that of your lover, too!"

Dear heaven, not Dylan, E.D. thought. Why hadn't she followed her own instincts and left when she should have?

"Trey, don't even think of playing that angle. He's a friend. I needed a place to stay when you threw me out of my own house. That's it."

"Keep those lies coming and I'll start phoning newspapers and TV stations to find out who'll offer me the most for this juicy story."

Incredulous, she shook her head. "You would do that to your own children? Hasn't Dani been through enough—and what has Mac done to deserve this notoriety and embarrassment?"

"You obviously didn't give a fig, why should I? At

least this way they'll get something out of it. You tell Judge Loverboy to be generous and I'll trade Dani's clunker of a car in for a sporty new model for her graduation. Won't she love her daddy then? And Mac can get the high-definition TV he's been salivating over."

"Buying their love with blackmail money? Trey, listen to yourself."

"What I want to hear is an answer," he all but snarled. "How long have you been cheating on me?"

"I never cheated on you!" she ground out. "I repeat, we are separated. I owe you no explanation as to what I do or don't do with my time."

"Not answering is as good as an admission of guilt." His abrupt laugh was hard-edged. "All those late nights at the office…those so-called business and charity events you got all gussied up for. It was all for him."

"That's not true," E.D. said with as much fury as fear for the man she loved. "I always asked you to come with me and you refused."

"You stopped asking ages ago."

And they said women were the illogical sex? E.D. shook her head in exasperation. "I got tired of entreating you to participate in something that was important to me."

"Yeah, well, we know that's the truth—it's all about *you*. You just wanted another chance to rub my face in how successful you were and what a failure I was. Well, you're going to pay, Ms. High and Mighty. And that includes the blood test I should get for my own peace of mind."

A gasp stopped E.D. from responding. Glancing around, she saw Dani on the stairs. From her stricken expression, E.D. knew she'd heard too much.

"Sweetheart," she said stepping toward her, "please don't pay attention to any of this. It isn't—"

"You're cheating on Daddy?"

"Dani—"

"Shut up!" Dani did an abrupt about-face and stomped back upstairs. "You liar—I never want to have to look at you again!"

Chapter Fourteen

*W*here are you?

As Dylan kept wondering, he used all resources at his disposal to find an answer—but E.D. had vanished.

They'd shared an exquisite night and morning together, culminating in a reluctant farewell with delaying kisses at her car. Then she'd laughingly shoved him to his SUV and had driven to work. The morning had held the promise of spring in all its flourishing rebirth and warmth. Dylan wished repeatedly throughout the day that they could have spent it together; however, she was buried in case study, while he had the drudgery of candidate commitments—appearances at parades and a few sentences expected here and there at various local events. He got through them all by fantasizing that next year E.D. would be at his side. Too soon, however, that ceased to subdue his growing concern about why she didn't return his calls.

By the usual close of office hours, Dylan was on the phone with Chris. "It's me," he said without preamble. "Has E.D. arrived yet?"

"Not that I know of, sir," Chris replied. "But I've just gotten in from the back section and haven't done more than check for phone messages. Want me to drive over to the cabin and make sure?"

Dylan suspected he was sounding like a nail-biting nanny or, worse, a stalker. "Thanks, I'm sure everything is okay. You take care of you and enjoy a cold one. I'll call later if I haven't figured this out."

He didn't resolve the mystery. At least not in the next hour, or the next...until Chris phoned him and told him that he'd used the master key to the cabin and found it empty. Empty of any evidence of E.D. Her clothes and luggage were gone.

After he hung up, Dylan sat in his condominium wondering how that could be. She'd left with her purse and briefcase in the morning, her eyes dreamy, her cheeks blooming from his kisses and whispered promises for tonight. How could there be nothing at the cabin now to show she'd ever been there, let alone would be returning? For one insane moment, as panic permeated his faith, he even worried that his trust in Chris had been badly placed. Just as quickly, shame had him rejecting that possibility. But that left him back where he'd begun.

Where have you gone? What have you done?

The litany began to sound like a bad ballad or worse, a requiem.

By nine o'clock, biting the bullet of pride, Dylan phoned Alyx Carmel. As much as he hated to do it, he figured if E.D. would contact anyone aside from him, it would be her divorce attorney. Alyx answered her phone.

"Hello, Judge. You held out longer than I suspected you would."

"I hope you made a bundle on the bet."

"That wasn't callous humor. Personally, this is breaking the heart I keep denying I have. If it helps any, I'm putting my money on you two."

Dylan took little comfort in that. "The odds don't look good if I don't know why she vanished or where she is. Apparently you do."

"Will it help to know she's safe…and that she did this for you?"

Sitting on the edge of the bed they'd shared last night, his elbows resting on his knees, he covered his eyes with his free hand. "Hell no. We went through all of this yesterday, Alyx. I assume she told you about the trespasser?"

"Yes."

"She gave me her word that she wouldn't do anything like this. The only reason she would break that promise is if something changed to force her. Now she's not even answering her cell phone. What changed, Alyx?"

"New pictures."

Thinking things couldn't get worse, Dylan discovered they could. He stared at the carpet but saw nothing but darkness. "Dani?"

"License plates…and a lovely remote cabin."

Dylan uttered a harsh expletive, then apologized.

Someone had wasted no time in digging his poison deeper under her skin. Because of *him*. She'd buckled, run a diversion—whatever the hell one could call it—for him.

"What hotel, Alyx?"

"Ask me something I can answer."

"She knows I'll start calling every one in the directory."

"She remembers you said you would and gave me a message to pass on. 'Please don't.'"

"Why should I believe that's from her? Are you really on her side, Alyx? Really? Something is dead-wrong ugly here and she's isolated now and all alone. Divide and conquer, get it? She needs me."

"Sorry, Judge. I'm not that much of a romantic."

"I don't believe you. Isn't love the summit all our souls reach for? Next stop, heaven? Ah, Alyx. Don't make me ring you every ten minutes tonight. Give me that number."

After a long pause, instead Alyx offered the name of the hotel in the next town north on the interstate. "At least I can deny giving you the number," she grumbled.

The bed was comfortable enough and the room was clean, so clean even the walls were bare except for the frameless mirror above the desk on the opposite wall. Still, E.D. couldn't have been more miserable as she paced the short distance from the door to the humming air conditioner under the double-wide window. She knew she could forget about sleep tonight and thought that had she been smart, she should have saved her money and returned to the office. But of course she couldn't do that because Dylan would have checked there.

Dylan... Her heart ached every time his name passed through her mind—which was nonstop. How he would hate her for doing this. She hadn't been able to bring herself to check how many phone messages there were on her cell phone for fear of weakening and calling him back. If she ever needed to be strong, it was now.

The knock at her door startled her. She glanced at the digital clock by the bed and saw that it was minutes away from ten o'clock. This motel chain didn't provide room service and she certainly hadn't ordered from the pizzeria across the parking lot. Biting her lower lip, she retraced her steps to peer through the security hole.

Dylan.

Alyx must have caved and told him which hotel, but even she didn't know what room. What's more, E.D. was on the second floor in the back of the building, while she'd parked her car up front. How on earth...?

Knowing he wouldn't go away, E.D. nervously unfastened both dead bolts and opened the door. As soon as she did, he stepped past her, went to the window and drew the heavy drapes closed.

"You saw me." Of course, she thought with chagrin as she closed the door.

"I saw you," he said returning to her.

He just stood there looking down at her, his hands at his sides, his expression volcanic with pent-up emotions—disappointment, hurt, anger, fatigue. Unable to bear it, she bowed her head in shame.

"Please understand," she whispered. "I had to do it."

"No, you didn't. What good did this do? He has the photos."

"We could claim he'd had them doctored."

"An expert can tell easily enough that they weren't."

"You can't be a part of my divorce, Dylan," she cried. "He's going to blackmail us or else charge adultery. It'll cost you the bench."

Her voice broke on that last word.

Muttering an oath, Dylan pulled her into his arms. "Don't. I'm trying like hell to be furious with you. If you cry, it's going to ruin everything."

With a shaky laugh, E.D. hid her face against his chest. He was still wearing the gray suit jacket he'd left in this morning, but had since removed the silver tie and released the top two buttons of his white shirt. She pressed her lips in that V and filled her hands with his jacket. Having convinced herself that she couldn't be near him—perhaps for a very long time—she couldn't keep from touching him.

"I love you," she whispered against his throat before kissing him there, as well.

"No, you don't," he muttered, stroking her hair. "You can't love someone and scare him to death, drive him insane with worry, torment him to where he's willing to break the law."

That last admission had her looking up at him. "What law were you thinking of breaking?"

"The one that would have had me kicking in that door if you didn't open it. Damn it, kiss me before I die from needing this."

And with that, he framed her face with his hands and locked his mouth to hers.

E.D. wanted his taste as hungrily as he seemed to want hers. Their tongues mated in feverish delight, only to withdraw so that their lips could nibble and suckle. Then the kiss deepened again, growing more insistent and yearning. So were their hands. He filled his with her hair one moment, then slid them down her back and restlessly to her hips to press her closer against his already strong arousal. She kneaded the tense muscles along his neck and in the next instant unbuttoned his shirt so she could score her nails against his hardened nipples.

Groaning, Dylan broke their kiss. "Put your mouth there," he pleaded between pants.

He needn't have asked, it was what she wanted and did. She loved the powerful tremor that rippled through his body, loved the soft hiss that he expelled through gritted teeth when she wet and licked him. Then she felt cooler air on her skin and realized he'd untied the belt of her black silk wraparound jacket to gain access to her breasts. He slipped his right hand into one lacy bra cup and the instant he brushed his thumb against her nipple, she grew damp with need.

With flawless direction, their mouths again locked, this time for a more desperate feeding. Their breathing growing shallow, they twisted out of their jackets, and he helped her with her bra. When she rubbed herself against his bared chest, he uttered another oath and flung the bedspread and most of the sheet off the bed with one strong tug.

A second later, E.D. found herself lying beneath him diagonally across the fitted sheet. They were less particular with the rest of their clothes. All they had patience for was to lower this and push aside that, until he could gain entry.

E.D. gasped as he filled her with his heat and strength. She arched her hips to get all of him and he filled his hands with her to that same end. It was too much, and yet not enough. Their thrusts were urgent, their breathless whispers incoherent pleadings of lust. They climaxed quickly and together, then clung to each other never wanting to let go again.

"That was too fast," Dylan said when he could speak.

"You can always try again."

She had a streak of wickedness he adored, using that oh, so polite tone when he knew she could still feel him pulsating inside her. "I plan to. It must have been the clothes that threw me off. There is something erotic about doing it when half-dressed."

"'Doing it.' How crass."

As she began to push at his shoulders, Dylan gave her earlobe a tiny nibble to keep her still. "With you, it is making love. Even when it's hot and desperate."

"I'm sorry I upset you," she said, turning her head to meet his gaze. "I can't believe I was so foolish."

"You thought you were protecting me. It's another of the things I cherish about you, though it also scares me to death," he added, brushing her hair off her shoulder to plant a kiss there. Reluctantly rolling off her, he finished kicking off the rest of his clothes, and more gently removed hers. Finally, he shifted both of them up to the pillows and tucked her against him. "You want to tell me about what happened?"

"You didn't grill Alyx?"

"All I wanted to hear from her was where you were hiding. I take it Trey was at the house when you arrived?"

"Yes, and I could immediately tell by his smirky smile that he was up to something."

Dylan tightened his arms around her. "You shouldn't have gone inside, darling. You know how often wives have gone missing or are found murdered at the hands of their estranged husbands."

"That crossed my mind, believe me."

E.D. then went on to give him a full recount of their conversation. With each nasty utterance from Trey's mouth, Dylan's fury grew. "How on earth could you ever have stayed married to that snake?" he groaned when she'd finished.

She sighed. "Frankly, he's never shown that side of himself—not to me and not to the kids. Oh, he could be sarcastic and abrupt when I tried to coax him into doing something he didn't want with the kids, and as I said, I stopped wanting him to attend functions with me long ago because I simply didn't care enough anymore." She glanced up at him. "The truth is that I was planning to leave him as soon as Mac made it to college."

Dylan uttered a deep growl. "That's years yet."

"I know, but I had no incentive. You were still married."

He had to kiss her for that. It filled him with immeasurable joy to know she'd always had feelings for him, too.

"I'm sorry about Dani witnessing that," he said, stroking her hair. "I know how much that hurts."

"It does." Sadness underscored her words. "But what hurts more is that I sensed she was also a little smug. I suspect she thinks this will get some of the heat off of her. As embarrassing as it is to admit, my daughter is a spoiled brat. I gave too much attention to my job and not enough to my children."

"E.D., I think most teens struggle with attitude at one point or another. And you can't possibly take all the blame. That was the point for Trey to be a stay-at-home dad. If anyone failed, he did."

"But instead of having to pay for that, he's going to fleece you as badly as he will me."

Dylan uttered a negative comment to that. "I'm not giving him so much as a nickel."

"You're going to let him go public with those pictures and accusations? Knowing what that will cost you?" she asked sitting up.

"If people are willing to believe lies over our truth, then I don't have the reputation I thought I did. I'll tell you what troubles me more—the 'who' behind those photos."

"Yes, I know." E.D. scored her lower lip with her teeth. "Has someone been out to get you or me all along? Trey called them 'a gift.' He wouldn't have done that if he'd been the one following us or if he'd hired a private detective to dig up some dirt to twist my arm."

"It wouldn't seem so."

"Then who?"

"If we could get hold of at least one of those photographs, I could probably get Jonas to check it out. Maybe the type of paper or the ink could give us a clue."

"I'm afraid I failed you again. Trey was sounding so crazy, I knew I had to get out of there. I didn't think he'd act like that if the kids were in the house."

"Mac never came downstairs?"

"No. He probably had his headphones on and missed the whole disaster. Thank goodness. I just hope Dani doesn't tell him. I couldn't bear it if he believed the worst in me."

Dylan stroked her cheek. "Don't do that to yourself. From what you told me about him, he worships you."

E.D. didn't look all that confident. "We need something to turn in our favor."

"I'm going to talk to Alyx first thing in the morning."

"About?"

"Someone ignored signs and came onto my property. I'm going to tell her that I'm picking up the fee for that guy she told you about who's supposed to be checking on Trey, and to tell him to give it his full attention."

"I can't see how that will help any. Apparently, he hasn't reported anything yet."

"He has to come upon something if he's on Trey's tail 24-7. That worm has been hitting a lucky streak because you refuse to play hardball for the sake of your kids."

"I hope you're right."

Wanting to get her mind off her parasite of a spouse and back onto him, Dylan let his fingers drift down her body to brush his knuckles over her left nipple. "Have I told you how amazingly beautiful you are?"

E.D.'s lips curved into a tender smile. "You do every time you look at me."

He slipped his hand around her waist and drew her over him. "I think I'm ready to improve upon my last performance," he murmured.

"I don't think that's possible, but if you insist…"

"Oh, I do," he rasped, and parted her lips with his.

Chapter Fifteen

"I'm sorry for being a bad friend."

With the exception of E.D., Dylan couldn't have wished for anyone to be on the opposite end of the phone more than Jonas Hunter. Belatedly flipping the calendar on his desk to Tuesday, he felt the strange shift of impetus inch toward his and E.D.'s side.

"You redeemed yourself just in time. That's a joke," he added in case his humor didn't translate fast enough. With the political atmosphere decidedly thin-skinned these days, he didn't want to take any chances with someone he truly wanted to brainstorm with.

"Relax, I got it. My excuse is that they've had me overseas—big hint, don't ask where or why—and the reward for that is a bit of breathing space. So tell me, how are things down there? I see you managed to stay out of the national headlines so far."

"You'd better knock wood fast. If the momentum around here gets any worse, we could be the lead story on the evening news."

Jonas grunted. "Dang, sorry for being a smart aleck. What's up and what can I do to help?"

"I'm not sure you have that much breathing space."

"Okay, how about I catch the next flight available and see if I can prove you wrong?"

"Call me when you land and don't bother with hotel reservations. I'll give you the key to my condo."

"And where will you be?"

"Not letting E.D. out of my sight."

"Mom? You gotta do something. I can't wear my head-phones much longer. I think fungus is attaching them to my ears, but Dani and Dad are really hard at it. Can you call me at lunch? I know you're in court. Try, okay?"

Try. The word out of her son's mouth had E.D. gulping down a myriad of emotions. And it was 12:55 p.m. The morning session had dragged beyond the most generous definition of endless and they had only begun a shortened lunch break ten minutes ago.

E.D. quickly dialed Mac's number, knowing the chances of catching him before he returned to class were minimal. Her wince turned into a grimace as she heard her call turned over to the message service. "Mac. I'm so sorry I missed you," she began. "Court only just recessed and apparently you're back in class. Mac—" she checked her words in case Trey got hold of her son's phone "—queen to knight, macaroni six to meatball three."

She disconnected, hoping she'd remembered their old secret code correctly. But she had followed her instincts, just as Dylan had worried she'd stopped doing. Mac needed out of the house. She was getting him out.

Her next call was to Dylan.

"The cavalry arriveth," Dylan said as he shook Jonas's hand and led him into his chambers. "Welcome back. For a guy who hates to fly, you sure are doing a bunch of it—even when you don't have to."

"I have an ulterior motive that I didn't tell you about. The possibility of another face-to-face with Alyx Carmel was too tempting to resist."

Dylan raised his eyebrows. "Well, now that's an interesting confession. Should I warn you that you have both the robe and building wrong? The confessional you need is two blocks down the road."

"Very funny, wise guy. Now put me to work."

"First we go to school."

Looking perplexed, Jonas watched Dylan hang up his robe and slip into his blue suit jacket. "School?"

"We have a passenger to pick up and deliver to the ranch."

Dylan explained things to Jonas on the drive across town. As expected, Jonas was none too happy to get caught in what could easily turn into an Amber Alert.

"There's one thing working in our favor," Dylan said, pulling into the long line of buses, cars and SUVs. "At their last meeting, Trey agreed to E.D.'s financial terms, withdrew the restraining order, and approved some visitation rights."

"Uh-huh. Including this one?"

"Look for a Harry Potter type–kid with lighter hair," Dylan said, avoiding that question.

"Does he know you?"

"No, but he knows to trust the message, 'queen to knight, macaroni six to meatball three.'"

That won Dylan a sidelong look. "Now you're telling me you've dug into our top-secret codes?"

Dylan chuckled. "It's something he and his mother dreamed up for security in case someone ever tried to convince him to go with a stranger."

"And you're willing to actually say that in broad daylight? In front of witnesses? Man, you have a serious case of it, don't you?"

"Yes, I do," Dylan said with a smile.

As students started pouring out of the school, Dylan spotted one that looked like the photo E.D. had shown him from her wallet. "I think we're set to go."

Despite knowing that Mac was safe and settled at Dylan's, E.D. was a bundle of nerves until she pulled into the ranch and saw her son come out of the cabin, a big grin on his face.

"Hey, mister," she said as she got out of the car.

"Mom, this place is so cool!"

"You like it here?" she asked with relief as she hugged her son. He'd never seemed the outdoors type and rarely lifted his head from his computer or a book.

But then neither she nor Trey had ever exposed their kids to the outdoors.

"There's this dog—"

"Lefty."

"Yeah, and he put his whole mouth around my wrist."

"Oh, boy." E.D. immediately checked her son's thin arm for wounds. Dylan had assured her that the dog was well trained.

"No, really. I never knew a dog with such big teeth could be so careful. See, Chris told him to show me their favorite fishing spot."

"Chris wouldn't have suggested the move if he didn't trust Lefty to be gentle," Dylan said as he came out to join them.

E.D.'s pulse accelerated as their gazes locked, and she so wanted to go into his arms. But she knew she needed to introduce Mac to their relationship slowly. "Thank you for doing this."

"My pleasure. Mac also called his father," he said with a speaking glance.

E.D. lifted Mac's chin to study his sweet, owlish face. "How did that go?"

The eleven-year-old shrugged and wrinkled his nose. "You know. He was pretty mad at me for telling."

"Well, I talked to him, too, and you don't have to worry that you'll hear any more about it." E.D. had phoned him right after she'd confirmed Dylan had Mac, and while Trey had threatened to send the police after her, she'd stood up to his threat. "Go ahead," she'd replied. "I'm sure they'll be interested in hearing Mac explain why he doesn't want to be at the house with those tirades between you and Dani going on." That had bought her a little time, although Trey hadn't been gracious about being outmaneuvered. E.D. had cut him short by promising to have Mac home in plenty of time in the morning to change and make it to school, then had disconnected.

"Mom! I met a real G-man, too!"

Startled, E.D. looked to Dylan for an explanation.

"Jonas managed some free time and flew down to help us brainstorm."

"I need to call Alyx. She's being coy when I've mentioned him to her, but I'll bet she won't complain when she hears he's here."

"Leave Alyx to Jonas," Dylan replied with a wink. "I dropped him off at his car and he should be with her now."

E.D. wanted to ask more, but knew she should wait until they were alone. "All right, then. I have picked up enough pizza to feed you guys, Lefty, Chris and all of the cattle on this place, so let's get inside before the cheese turns into concrete."

It was almost an hour before she and Dylan could be alone and talk. Chris seemed pleased to be invited to join them and with touching consideration had just repaid the gesture by offering to show Mac the stables and get him started on learning how to ride.

"Homework done, young man?" E.D. asked her elated son.

"Yes, ma'am. Judge Justiss let me use his computer. Thank you again, sir."

"You're very welcome. Enjoy yourself. Chris is part magician when it comes to horses."

As soon as they left with Lefty leading the way, Dylan rose from his chair at the kitchen table and drew E.D. out of hers. "At last," he murmured, gathering her close.

With every day, each gesture of sensitivity and compassion he displayed, E.D. fell deeper in love with him. He didn't have to coax her to meet his kiss; she had been waiting for this since he'd agreed to help her rescue Mac.

"Why is it that the more clothes you put on, the stronger my desire is to peel them off?" he breathed, finally working a series of kisses across her cheek to the sensitive spot beneath her ear.

As his hands roamed under her jacket to span her waist, then strayed upward to determine what bra she wore today, E.D. laughed softly. "Then I can't wait for winter."

"Me, either. I'm for any excuse to snuggle." Kissing her again, he added tenderly, "How's the case going?"

Her smile waned. "The defense is pounding away. Surviving this one will be about faith and tenacity, in that order."

"At the worst time. My precious E.D. I'll help with the faith part." With a glance out the patio doors, his expression grew provocative. "Want to sit on the patio swing and practice our future?"

Who would be crazy enough to refuse an offer like that? She gripped his hand and kissed him again.

The afternoon was growing steamy with the promise of overnight thunderstorms. Even so, E.D. sighed with contentment to be shoulder to thigh with Dylan on the swing. Resting her head on his shoulder, she could easily imagine a time where this would be part of their regular schedule. Then images of Dani clouded her vision.

"This fighting between Trey and Dani—it's new."

"You mean she's always been a daddy's girl?"

"No, she's always been independent." E.D. didn't like her growing concerns regarding her eldest child. "I'm not sure she's anyone's girl. I think she's gauging who's in the best position at the end to aid her personal ambitions and will align herself accordingly. Mac's recounts of those arguments while you were inviting Chris over tells me she's not happy with something she's seen or heard. What I need to hear are details. My *dilemma* is that she doesn't want to speak to me."

"That's got to hurt like hell." Dylan tightened the arm he had around her shoulders.

"If it wasn't for the demands of my job, and you, I don't think I could have stood it."

"I wish I knew of a solution or could do more."

"Bless you for that."

After a slight pause, Dylan asked, "Do you think Mac will learn to like or at least accept me?"

That question kicked in E.D.'s most tender instincts. Of course, Dylan had to be experiencing his own vulnerability in all of this. He had to wonder if her feelings for him would stay as strong if her children rejected him.

"I think he already respects you—and is awed by you. Good grief, attorneys are a dime a dozen. You're a *judge*. He's heard me discuss court enough to realize the achievement in that, as well as the responsibility in the position." E.D. shot him a mischievous look. "I've also told him how you're one of the top dogs and going to be seated even higher soon."

Dylan chuckled. "Top dog. Well, that's bound to impress him."

Glad to make him laugh and feel him relax, she continued gently, "Is this a good time to warn you that I'll be spending the night on the couch?" While she had total confidence in his ability to win over her son, she wanted to give Mac time to adjust to how intimate their relationship had become.

"You wouldn't be you if you'd told me otherwise," he said, his gaze admiring. "But you take the bed, I'll take the couch."

"You're too tall for the couch, and if Mac has a breathing episode, he can crash on the other one, reassured that I'm close. There's no reason for all of us to have a disrupted night."

"What if I feel like peeking in on you to take parenting notes?"

E.D. shook her head in bemusement. "If you get any more perfect, I'll have to worry that you'll be kidnapped because women everywhere will want to harvest your DNA for cloning."

They both laughed, but just as quickly she grew serious as she considered the ominous clouds rising in the western sky. It was impossible not to.

"Ah, Dylan…" she sighed. "I believe there's another storm coming, worse than what we'll see tonight."

There was no delay in the kiss that Dylan pressed to

her forehead. "You think that scares me? The idea of not knowing where you are when I open my eyes is far worse. I'll be here, E.D. No matter what comes, I'll be here."

Chapter Sixteen

The weather was rough overnight, and Mac's asthma did give him a difficult hour or so, probably a reaction due to not being used to hay or horses. E.D. concluded the excitement of riding and playing with Lefty had to have contributed to things, too. But she was a veteran of these episodes and was at his side in a heartbeat after hearing his distress, then stayed with him to gauge how bad it was and whether medical help would be needed. It struck her that in the morning she would have to talk to Dylan. If he wanted them here, they would need to have some equipment for Mac because the nearest hospital was some distance away. Not doing so would be taking an unacceptable risk.

As another flash of lightning lit the living room, she saw Dylan watching them from the hallway. Seconds later the house vibrated from the latest peal of long-rolling thunder. The image of him filling that entryway looking ever so sexy in a dark-colored terry-cloth robe did something similar to her insides.

"Some storm, huh?" she murmured, continuing to gently rub Mac's back as his breathing continued to progress toward normal. "I wondered if you'd be able to sleep."

"I heard Mac first, but didn't want to intrude."

When he remained in the entryway, E.D. extended her free hand to him. "You aren't."

Dylan settled on the edge of the coffee table, took her hand and lightly kissed her fingers. "How's he doing?"

"Much better. He'll be completely asleep in another minute."

"I should never have recommended the riding."

"No, he loved it. Don't blame yourself. Besides, it's important for him to try to have as normal a life as possible." With the next flash of lightning, E.D. glanced at her watch on the other side of the coffee table. "What time is it?" She didn't have a clue.

"Just past midnight." Dylan reached out to stroke her hair. "You've got to be dead on your feet. Go take the bed. I'll watch him."

"That's sweet, but he's okay now." She rose from the couch and adjusted the sheet over Mac.

Drawn by the pounding rain on the roof, she went to the window to draw aside the sheer drapes. "I'm glad the hail was pea size and lasted only seconds."

Coming up behind her, Dylan wrapped his arms

around her waist, gently urging her to lean against him. "I'll look into having a carport built. I don't know why I haven't before. I guess it's because I didn't spend as much time here, so there was no real need."

E.D. couldn't help but feel a little thrill that he was already making plans for their future. If only that future could begin tomorrow.

"Brenda preferred being in town?" she asked, keeping her voice as quiet as he did.

"Pretty much."

When he nuzzled her ear with his nose, E.D. understood he didn't want to talk about her. Someday she would explain that she didn't mind, that she accepted Brenda's claim on those early years.

"Cute jammies."

Actually they were nothing more than cotton gym shorts and a large University of Texas T-shirt. "Sexy robe...or rather sexy man in the robe."

"I'll stop at nothing to tempt you."

"That doesn't take much effort where you're concerned."

Before Dylan could respond, lightning flashed again. He grunted and urged her away from the window. "No need to ask for trouble. Do you think Mac would mind if I sat with you on the couch?"

"These episodes wear him out. He'll sleep hard now until I wake him in the morning." Which would be brutally early considering all that they needed to do and not make him late for class. Just thinking about that had E.D. fighting a yawn.

Dylan settled in a corner of the couch and put his feet

on the coffee table, then he coaxed her into half sitting and half lying against his chest. "Close your eyes."

"You can't be comfortable."

"Wanna bet?

E.D. wasn't about to argue with him, even if she had the energy. She'd been lonely for him and loved that he didn't want to leave her. With a peaceful sigh, much like the one Mac had uttered a moment ago, she yielded to the pull of sleep.

"Don't you ever answer your messages?"

E.D. closed her hours log and, leaning back in her chair, she gripped the desk phone's receiver more tightly. Hearing Alyx's excited and agitated voice had her thoughts immediately shifting away from work. She had checked her cell-phone messages at every opportunity on Thursday wondering why she hadn't heard from her. Perhaps that was naive, but she'd thought with Jonas Hunter's experience and clout, there would be some news about something. Now Friday was half-over, too, and she was about to open the bag lunch she'd picked up on her way from court.

"I did, not fifteen minutes ago," she told the other attorney. "What's up?"

"How soon can you get here?"

E.D. sat forward. "You mean your office?" This was not what she'd expected to hear. "You've got to be kidding. Even though court has recessed until Monday, I have a credenza stacked with work to deal with before I dare leave this office today."

"What if I told you that Dylan is already on his way?"

Dylan had a light court day scheduled, but was being pestered to do more campaign-related appearances. He was too responsible not to honor them.

E.D.'s suddenly dry mouth had her eyeing the iced tea on her desk with longing. "This is important, isn't it?"

"It's huge—and don't ask me to say any more than that."

"I'm on my way," E.D. told her, already out of her chair.

When she arrived at Alyx's office twelve minutes later, she found Dylan standing over Alyx's desk, his expression granite-hard, while the divorce attorney was in full peripatetic mode, looking as if she was close to wearing out the soles of her shoes if not the carpet.

"Where's Jonas?" E.D. expected to see him here, as well. Dylan hadn't said anything about him returning to Washington, D.C.

"Keeping tabs on two-thirds of our triangle," Alyx said with a cold smile. "My guy is tailing the other one."

"Triangle?" E.D. didn't understand, but when Dylan extended his hand to her, she approached the desk. That was when she realized what he'd been looking at. "Oh, God. Not more photographs."

She didn't want to look. What had Trey managed to get this time? Dylan kissing her senseless in the car the morning they'd left the hotel?

Although her stomach was edging dangerously close to her throat, she took Dylan's hand and squeezed hard. "I don't think I can do this."

He gave her the support of his arm around her shoulders. "You've got through the hard part, the hurtful part. Now it's time to get angry…and then get justice."

Everyone was speaking in riddles, E.D. thought, shaking her head. Sighing, she let her gaze drop to the photographs…and a moment later her mouth fell open in a soundless gasp.

Catching her expression, Alyx uttered a harsh laugh. "Trey the homebody…Trey the introvert…Trey the victim. Oh, I am *so* going to enjoy calling his attorney."

Barely paying attention, E.D. tried to wrap her mind around what she was looking at and what it all meant. In the first photo there were Trey and Giselle, Dani's dance teacher, exiting the studio together, he with a proprietary hand at the small of her back. Then there was the photo where Trey leaned across a restaurant table, this time his hand covering hers and his expression one of undisguised male hunger. The last in the first row was of a house—apparently Giselle's—and Trey was clearly delaying his departure by kissing Giselle passionately.

No wonder Dylan's expression had been stony.

With helpless curiosity, she continued her examination of the next row of photographs. Giselle again with someone E.D. didn't recognize. She frowned at the equally dark-haired man. He stood only inches taller than the petite dance instructor did and he was no less good-looking in the same flashy kind of way. At first E.D. thought he might be an adult ballroom student, since the photo was of them dancing, and he had the build and posture. But she was in for a huge shock when in the last photo he was in a park with Giselle where he had the woman so tightly pressed against a tree trunk that she either was in danger of swallowing his tongue or of getting permanently tattooed by bark.

Without looking up, she asked Alyx, "Who is he?"

"Geoffrey Post."

E.D. started a vague, "I don't know any—"

"Post Photography Studio."

The photographer! This was the man who had taken those awful photos of her daughter. She had to clench her hand to keep from grabbing up the photo and tearing it to shreds, the way she would like to tear into that piece of slime.

He was Giselle's lover?

Giselle was also Trey's lover.

Dear heaven, E.D. thought, her vision momentarily blurred as one part of her mind worked in overdrive drawing conclusions, while another part challenged new questions. Whatever she'd imagined, this was far worse.

"How could Trey be having an affair with her? He knows she recommended this Geoffrey Post, knows that Dani would take guidance from her and trust her opinion."

"Maybe she didn't know about the photos," Alyx offered, playing devil's advocate.

E.D. remembered the dance-school teacher's private smile at the hospital. There was something about it that had bothered her, but too much had been happening for E.D. to keep it in the forefront of her mind. "She knew," she decided. "She has to. It's clear she knows how many teeth he has in his mouth," she added with a disdainful nod at the intimate photo.

To think Trey had the nerve to treat E.D. as though she had the morals of an alley cat when all the time the snake had been playing her for a fool. The question begged how long had this been going on? Dani had been taking lessons since she was Mac's age. E.D. thought if she discovered that the affair had that longevity, she would dump every piece of paper in Trey's office out onto the front yard and set a match to the pile. Damn his hide, she might regardless.

"I'm sorry, darling," Dylan said in a voice that was for her ears only. "Why don't you sit down? You'd make a ghost look tanned."

"Tell me the rest. Everything." She looked up at him. "Do you know?"

"They're still trying to dig up details and put it all together," he said grimly. He glanced at Alyx. "Tell her what else you've accomplished."

"Well, with Jonas able to keep an eye on Mr. Post, my investigator got most of those photos, and copious notes about times, locations, et cetera, so there should be no problem getting receipts and testimony to cut a fairer divorce settlement, or for your case against Geoffrey Post."

"Oh, there will be no divorce settlement," E.D. seethed. "The question is whether Trey will be alive to plead nolo contendere."

"Now, E.D.," Alyx warned, "you've won the war. There's no reason to sacrifice your own freedom, not to mention your future, for a moment of passionate outrage, justified as you would be."

E.D. didn't need the warning; rather it helped to voice the depth of her contempt. "Okay, so you have photos and documentation. What about motivation? Did Post or Giselle single out Dani for the photos? What else were they planning for her?"

"Those are questions a criminal attorney will be asking. In the meantime, Jonas has been putting a fire under the local FBI office to build a federal case against Post. After significant investigation, it would appear he has had a few brushes with the law in three other states, and all of them involving either blackmail, lewd behavior with an underage female, or—"

"No more." E.D. pressed her hand to her stomach, afraid she was going to embarrass herself. "I have to go talk to Dani. If I learn he's done more than take photos, if he's—I'll want him arrested today!"

Dylan put a calming hand on her shoulder. "You can't go over there. If Trey learns you know about his affair—"

"And who knows what else," E.D. ground out.

"Actually, Trey's not at the house," Alyx interjected. "He's having a nooner with Ms. Healthy Hormones."

"He could return at any time," Dylan all but growled back. "It's not safe."

"I told you, he's being watched. We can have them buzz E.D.'s cell phone."

That clearly wasn't good enough. "I'll go with you," Dylan told E.D.

Raising her hands for them to stop, E.D. said, "That

will put Dani on the defensive and she'll think all the lies her father told her are true and that I'm just trying to get back at him."

"Are you sure? Remember Mac said they're having constant yelling matches."

"Yes, but Dani thinks the world is against her right now, and we now know Trey has reason to be on edge himself." To Alyx she said, "Are these the only copies you have?"

"They're on a disk. Take what you need."

Nodding her thanks, E.D. scooped up the whole set. "I'll keep my phone on," she assured Dylan quietly. "If I get word that he's headed back, I'll get out of the house."

"What makes you think Dani isn't likely to do something crazy and reckless? E.D., please," he entreated. "I couldn't bear it if you were wrong about this move."

"If something happens that I have to call 9-1-1, the media will be there in seconds. You can't be anywhere near there."

"Hell, you're more important to me than an election."

"So are you," she said with a sad smile.

Leaving Dylan frowning in confusion, she hurried for the door.

Chapter Seventeen

For all her determination, E.D. didn't know if Dani would open the door to her. But she had one hope in case the girl refused. When they weren't estranged, she and Trey would keep a key in the back by the patio tucked behind the wall thermometer. Although the locks were now changed, she hoped her kids' ability to forget or misplace their own keys had compelled Trey to continue the arrangement.

Nerves were taking their toll on her, and a quick call to the office to warn her secretary and Bruce that she would be out for a personal emergency didn't help. Bruce told her that Emmett had been asking for her.

"Cover for me as well as you can," she directed. "But don't put your own neck in a noose, promise?"

"It's not like you don't deserve a break," he replied

with open sympathy. "I'm just sorry there's another problem for you. Take care and let me know if there's something I can do."

The neighborhood was quiet as E.D. turned into Yucca Lane. To her relief she didn't pass one neighbor—she assumed by now word had spread up and down the street and then some about the pending divorce as much as Dani's situation. Thankfully, the driveway was also empty.

After parking, E.D. went to the front door and rang the doorbell. She couldn't hear anything from inside like a TV or stereo, but she knew Dani could easily be wearing headphones and not hear her, either.

Just when she was about to try the backyard, she heard a turn of a dead bolt. Then the steel gray-and-red door swung open.

"What are you doing here?"

Dani wasn't being her most sullen or rude, in fact it seemed she was actually curious. Hopeful, E.D. took a deep breath to keep her own tested emotions in check.

"I was concerned for you. You may be hearing some news soon, maybe within hours, and I wanted you to be forewarned in case the phone starts ringing again. May I come in for a moment?"

Dani looked surprised by the request and took a few seconds to weigh—or enjoy—the power in that. Then with a one-shouldered shrug she let go of the doorknob and walked down the foyer toward the kitchen. "Suit yourself."

The sight of her daughter's condition disturbed E.D. anew. Gone was the lithe, immaculate ballerina with her blond hair impeccably coifed in a bun or braid, and her makeup subtle but enhancing her delicate features. There were no words that fit her now save the one too often applied to teenagers—*slob*. The girl's hair was loose, lank and clearly needing a shower—like the rest of her. She had yet to change out of her nightshirt and it had ketchup and chocolate syrup stains on it. There were times E.D. worried when Dani didn't eat; however, this wasn't one of them. There was no missing that the girl was bingeing on food and not working out—the results were weight gain. It all reflected a loss of self-esteem and—as much as the girl tested her devotion—broke E.D.'s heart.

Closing the door, she followed her daughter to the kitchen. Dani already had the refrigerator open and was pretending to browse. It was all E.D. could do not to ask her to please stop wasting energy and shut it.

"Where's your father, dear?" she asked instead.

"I don't know and I can't say that I care."

"Mac said things were difficult here."

Dani slammed the door. "What else did that tattle-tale say?"

"He didn't rat on you, Dani, or your father. He just couldn't block out the noise even with headphones and knew he needed a break. I suspect if I go next door, I can probably learn more than what he told me." E.D. put her purse on the counter. "Please, I don't want to fight. I want to help because I know you're feeling totally abandoned. I know your father is increasingly away from home and you think he doesn't feel badly for you."

Dani frowned. "He's probably looking for a job.

With you holding out on him, he doesn't even have money to go to the supermarket. Take a look in the refrigerator if you don't believe me."

The girl was so miserable, she was waffling between wanting to make peace with one of them, but not sure whom. It was time to give her another heads-up. "He's not looking for a job, honey, and he has money. I've already signed over a considerable amount so that he can keep things normal for you and Mac."

"Things aren't normal. They'll never be normal again."

That was true enough, E.D. thought with mixed emotions. "Okay, so they won't be exactly like what you thought you knew and wanted, but positives can come out of that."

"I don't see how."

Sensing she wanted reassurance, E.D. knew she first had to take away the last of Dani's misguided beliefs and trust. "I have something to show you," she said gently. "It's going to be painful, but you need to see so that you understand I was duped and betrayed as much as you were."

Hoping she was doing the right thing, E. D. took out the photos and spread them on the counter for Dani to view. As she'd expected—as she'd *hoped*—the girl was stunned. At least that told her that Dani hadn't realized about Trey and Giselle.

"Oh, my God," she keened. "I don't believe this. Where did you get these?"

"A private detective…and an FBI agent."

"FBI!"

Now she had the teen's attention.

Wrapping her arms around her waist, Dani looked as sick as E.D. had felt when she'd first seen the photos. "That's…that's disgusting!"

And yet she continued to stare at them as though hypnotized…only not so much the photos of her father with Giselle. Narrowing her eyes, E.D. eased around the counter to be certain.

"Dani…did you know your father was having an affair with Giselle?"

"Of course not," the girl huffed.

"If you did, and you still accused me of infidelity, I wouldn't know what to say. You actually believe I would betray my marriage and our family? Compromise the family's livelihood?"

"How would your affair do that?"

Her phrasing grated as much as her continuing to think only of herself. "While I lived in this house, Dani, while I was your father's wife, I did not betray my vows or his trust. Clearly, he can't make the same claim."

Dani chewed on her lower lip that was already raw and bloodied. "Mac says you brought him to a ranch and the guy who owns it is a judge who's in love with you."

E.D. had given her son permission to be honest, but had asked him to refrain from mentioning Jonas or personal conversations. "The judge has always been a professional friend—that's all, and I'll swear on the stand if need be. You know how seriously I take oaths.

"Now, when your father humiliated me and blamed your photos as something I allowed, never mind caused, then evicted me from my own home, I needed a place to stay. The judge lives in the city, but, yes, as Mac said, he offered me the use of his cabin."

"So he's not in love with you?"

"Yes, he is. He lost his wife to cancer, but he would never have said anything if this hadn't happened and he'd believed your father and I were happy."

Dani shot her a mature, knowing look. "You haven't been happy in a long while. You pretend to be. Dad barely bothered."

Wincing, E.D. took a risk and touched Dani's arm. "I'm sorry. I'd hoped I'd seemed reassuring so that you'd know that regardless of what was deteriorating in our marriage, you and Mac were my priority."

Discreetly glancing at her watch and seeing how time was quickly passing, E.D. was relieved that at least her phone hadn't buzzed a warning yet, but she knew she needed to get to the hard questions before Trey's return. "So what is most disgusting about those photos?" she asked, all but holding her breath for the expected 180-degree turn in her daughter's behavior.

Her daughter remained silent.

"I see. Well, will you at least have the decency to finally tell me who signed the authorization for the modeling shoot because you and I both know it wasn't me."

Dani glared down at the photos. "Giselle."

It should have felt better to know, but it didn't. It stung bitterly—not for Trey's betrayal, but for trusting that over-painted witch with her only daughter's future. "Did you ask her to do it?"

"No." Dani was fast and firm with that reply. "When

she suggested I start building a portfolio to show modeling studios, that it could help defer college expenses, I told her that you'd never go along with anything like that while I was in high school and a minor. She said while I was dragging my feet, another girl with my looks would get the jobs I should get. She said the photographer she recommended had helped two other girls sign with big names."

"But you don't want to be a model, Dani—at least you never said you did."

"Not really. He was going to do the shoot for free, though. And if I did get some modeling jobs, the money would be nice."

Dani didn't realize she'd tripped herself up again. When she'd first mentioned the photos in passing, they were to be for some production at the dance studio, leaving E.D. to conclude all the girls would be included and packets would be sent home for possible purchase. It was increasingly clear that the sneaky teen had seen a way to go away to college with an allowance from home *and* some serious mad money.

She'd been lured by the "something for nothing," promise. E.D. groaned to herself. Adults fell for that every day of the week, so why shouldn't a kid who had yet to know how to balance a checkbook?

"Sadly, you learned a painful lesson and discovered it *did* cost you something," she said.

"It's her fault," Dani muttered, continuing to give Giselle's image a venomous look. "I'll bet she swiped those photos from him and put them on the Internet herself."

"Why would she do that when she brought you to him in the first place?"

"Because she's jealous of me!"

E.D. had ceased being able to navigate through her daughter's thinking. This was *not* the justification for Dani's behavior that she'd expected, or wanted, to hear. "Pardon me, I think I lost you. Are you suggesting Giselle saw you as a professional threat? She's my age, and that's a little late to begin a modeling career. I don't think she could even compete with someone your age trying out for a Broadway chorus line."

With a surprising pride, Dani lifted her chin. "You're not usually this obtuse, Mother. I *said* she had a crush on Geoff and realized he was more interested in *me*."

Poor, poor blind girl. Gently, E.D. asked, "Is that why you did those poses? You thought it would make him stay interested in you?"

"He said he was falling in love with me and that we'd be together once I graduated."

"A man in love doesn't take illegal pictures of a girl young enough to be his daughter. A man in love doesn't leave you and go do that with another woman," E.D. added pointing to the park scene. She gestured to the entire collection. "Take a harder look, Dani—you're not in any of these photos. It's all about Giselle."

Giselle Garza had been a busy woman, a clever woman; too bad she'd wasted those street-smart wits of hers on emotionally corrupting and pimping for a deviant. Well, E.D. thought with some small satisfaction, Giselle had met someone she couldn't hoodwink, and if she didn't have an arrest sheet yet, E.D. would see she began one, at least for the charge of forgery to commit—

Suddenly E.D. faced her daughter with new dread. "Dani…did you have sex with Geoffrey Post?"

"No."

"Please be honest with me. I'm looking out for *you,* your health to be more specific." They'd had the safe-sex talk a couple of years ago when the statistics had warned E.D. that kids were starting younger and younger, and had some disturbing definitions of what even constituted "sex." "If you have," she continued, "well, that's done, isn't it? But if you didn't practice safe sex—"

"We didn't do it! He said he respected me too much and that he could wait."

It was one thing to hear such inane declarations from a stranger on the stand; to hear her own flesh and blood declare it with such conviction rocked E.D. to her core, and muted what relief she felt regarding the sex. The one thought that kept coming back with glaring persistence was *How have I failed you?*

"Thank you for finally explaining this to me," she said, her heart heavy. "I guess the only other question I need to ask you at the moment is if you've been in touch with him since all this hit the fan?"

"No."

She sounded dejected enough to be telling the truth—and to leave E.D. with the concern that if he did contact her, she would run to him like the silly bunny that she was. "Do you really believe yourself in love with him?"

Her daughter glanced down at the photographs with growing loathing. "I wouldn't have her leftovers. She can keep him. She can have my father, too!"

Bursting into tears, Dani ran out of the kitchen and down the hall. About to follow her, E.D.'s phone buzzed in her purse. As she grabbed it and flipped it open, she didn't recognize the number, but took the call anyway.

"Yes?"

"He's on his way home," Jonas said, all business. "If you're planning on leaving you'd better do it fast."

"As tough as this conversation was, no blood has been shed so far. I'd like to get through this discovery in one afternoon if I could."

After a brief hesitation he said, "How about some backup then?"

Not again. The man was a dear, but relentless. "I told Dylan to stay away, Jonas. Maybe you can get him to resist committing professional suicide. He won't listen to me."

"I mean me, E.D. People tend to get very temperate and polite when I flash my badge." When she hesitated, Jonas cleared his throat. "I'd take it as a personal favor if you'd allow me this opportunity to assist. I promise anything I hear aside from legal issues that may relate to the Bureau will be forever flushed into the scary wasteland of my memory."

After what she'd been through in the last hour, it should have been impossible to smile, but E.D. almost managed. "Thank you, Jonas. Under those circumstances, I'd be grateful for your support."

"Well, then, see you in about three minutes."

Chapter Eighteen

It didn't take long for E.D. to be grateful that Jonas Hunter had talked her into adding his presence for this next conversation.

She decided to be waiting at the front door when Trey pulled into the driveway. One look at his flushed face and the way he thrust out his lower lip like an irate bulldog, and she could tell he intended to be aggressive from the start.

All that changed when a silver sedan pulled up behind him, effectively blocking him in.

"What the hell…?" Trey began doing a double take.

"Mr. Sessions—" as Jonas walked up the driveway, he smoothly pulled out his leather case and flipped it open to expose his badge and photo ID. "Special Agent Jonas Hunter, Federal Bureau of Investigation. Please, feel free to continue on inside, sir. No need to attract any more attention than is necessary."

"What business do you have with me?" Trey said, slightly less confident than before.

"That's what Ms. Martel and I are here to determine."

Trey pivoted on his heel and with fists clenched, he strode the rest of the way up the drive and walkway. As he reached E.D., he tilted his head back in order to look down his nose at her. "What kind of joke do you think you're playing now?"

Noting his words were slightly slurred, she didn't bother replying to that; rather, she led the way to the kitchen.

"How did you get in? She sure wouldn't have opened the door."

Every time he opened his mouth, he drifted farther away from the man she'd believed he'd been—bright, charming and as committed to family as she was. "The fact is she did. And we had an enlightening talk."

E.D. had stopped at the kitchen counter and had turned to face him as she responded. Now she stepped aside so that he couldn't help but notice the photos. Over his shoulder, she saw Jonas, who stayed in the doorway, his camel-colored suit jacket unbuttoned, his hands lightly clasped before him. She knew why the jacket was open, why he stood with his feet slightly parted, why— except for a brief wink—he kept his gaze on Trey. She just hoped Trey hadn't had so much to drink that he didn't grasp how outmatched he was, on every level.

"You showed her...this?"

"She had a right to know, and I had a right to answers."

He stood there taking in each photo, his color rising, his breathing growing rapid. "You've been having me tailed? And never said anything?"

It became increasingly clear to E.D. where Dani inherited her concept of logic. "The idea is not to conduct oneself in a manner that begs surveillance, Trey. But I do get your point. You're not sorry are you? You're sorry you got caught."

He shoved his hands into the pockets of his Dockers and avoided her steady gaze. "It's not like that. We didn't go out until you left."

"These aren't the only photos," she said on a bluff. "And I didn't leave, Trey. I was evicted from my own home, accused of the most horrendous things and humiliated at my office, in court, and on TV." When he opened his mouth to defend himself, E.D. raised her hand to stop him. "Dani confessed that your girlfriend signed that authorization for her."

Trey all but whined, "She told me you did."

"Oh, yes, I know our daughter has some serious problems with the truth, but apparently so does Giselle. But she would never have risked it if she wasn't confident she had you right where she wanted you." She looked down at the photos pretending to contemplate. "She seems to like to go from one of you to the other. Where do you think she is now?"

"You don't have to rub it in," he said, wiping his damp upper lip with the back of his hand. "Damn her."

"My thoughts exactly," E.D. said, preparing for her summation. "But don't worry, she's not going to get away with all of it. On the other hand, it's a pity we can't do even that much to you for your blind lust. You'll just have to live with knowing you'd have to share Giselle with Geoffrey Post, just like she intended Dani to share handsome Geoff with her."

Trey sounded as if he was choking. In the next instant, he uttered a harsh curse and swept the photos off the counter. Gasping, he collapsed onto the nearest bar stool.

Jonas took a step toward him, but E.D. gave him a quick negative shake of her head.

"Giselle wouldn't have done that," he said as though trying to convince himself. "She isn't that—"

"Twisted? Perverse? Sick?"

Trey rubbed his face "What happens now?"

This checkmate gave her no pleasure; at the same time she felt only contempt for her estranged husband. "Nothing is more important than getting Dani psychiatric help. She also goes to summer school. If for some reason you're still besotted with Ms. Garza, under no circumstances do you allow that woman any access to Dani."

"Don't worry, I won't be seeing her again."

"I wasn't worried, I was making you a promise." She waited until Trey's nod indicated he followed. "If Dani straightens up and takes her therapy sessions seriously, *I'll* find her another dancing school.

"One more thing—you don't fight me regarding custody of the kids."

He looked dazed. "You'll turn them against me."

"You're managing fine without any assistance from me." Reaching for her purse, E.D. slipped the strap over her shoulder. "I won't stop them from seeing you if that's what they want and you promise never to get drunk when they're here."

"You're still giving me the house?"

She couldn't wait to get out herself. "This is the house they were born in, and they'll need a place to stay if they visit. "

"Thank you," he said as though the words were being pulled out of him.

"Don't thank me, try and become worthy of the gesture."

Stepping around the photos, she paused by Jonas. "Give me five minutes to go and check on Dani. I need to know that she isn't apt to hurt herself again."

It was heartening to find the door unlocked, but Dani was facedown on the bed and very still.

E.D. sat on the edge of the rumpled sheets and laid a hand on her daughter's back. "Can I get you anything before I go?"

"No. Thanks."

"Dani, your father's home. We've talked. There are going to be big changes made, but it won't all be smooth sailing. You'll hate some of what I'll ask of you."

"So what else is new?"

"Could you please sit up? This is something you need to hear."

At first E.D. thought the girl was going to ignore the request, but then she flipped onto her back, and crabwalked herself against the headboard. "I'm listening."

"Thanks. I just needed you to know that what happened didn't only affect your future, it's going to have lasting reverberations in all our lives."

"But it happened to *me*."

"And your conduct reflects on me, meaning I will probably never run for the D.A.'s job after all."

Dani frowned. "It's what you worked so hard to get."

"I did work hard. The problem is a campaign isn't about the person best deserving and befitting a position, it's about many other things, including what baggage he or she brings to the office. Inevitably, the press would bring up this episode again, and aside from the concern of withstanding such a grilling on my conduct and failed responsibility to you—I would never ask you to go through another day of this again. A job isn't worth it."

"You would do that for me?"

"For you, for all of us." Because she knew what mattered most to her now. "As for your career aspirations, I promise, if you'll work with me, I will help you fulfill the potential I have always believed you possessed."

Her daughter glanced toward the door. "I don't want to stay here with him."

"For the time being that's how it has to be, as we work out logistics and everything, but you can call me at any time, just like Mac does, and I'll be coming back regularly to check on you."

"Can I get riding lessons like Mac did?"

"I'm sure that's something that can be arranged if you apply yourself to your final class work and show that you can be trusted again not to abuse privileges."

The girl sighed as though she were being asked to copy the *History of the Roman Empire* in calligraphy.

E.D. patted Dani's bare leg. "Now how about you head for the shower and change the sheets on this bed. They look and smell like they can walk themselves to the washing machine. Will you do that for me? I know it will make you feel better."

"Okay. I am pretty sick of myself."

When E.D. closed the front door of the house behind her, she paused to tilt her head up to the warm spring sunshine and closed her eyes to absorb the moment of peace. She had no illusions that things would be all smooth sailing from here on, but with the help of good people and a man she could count on, she knew they had as much of a chance as anyone to succeed. That was all they needed—a chance.

Realizing she wasn't with him, Jonas paused at the driveway and glanced back at her. "Okay, E.D?"

"Mm. Fine."

"Looks like we have company."

Shading her eyes with her hand, she noticed the SUV parked behind Jonas's rent-a-car and with a wry smile shook her head. "I should have known he wouldn't stay away."

"At least he didn't break the door down," Jonas drawled. He gave Dylan a thumbs-up sign.

As for E.D., she blew him a kiss and promised herself that she would improve on that when they were finally alone again.

She could hardly wait.

Epilogue

On an enjoyably mild Austin, Texas, morning in January, Judge Dylan Justiss took the oath of office to sit on the state's court of appeals. Holding his family bible passed down through generations was E.D. Martel-Justiss, his bride of four months.

Dylan was hard-pressed to focus on what he was supposed to repeat with his beloved and beautiful Eva Danielle reducing his thoughts to confetti. He still couldn't believe she was his. One of the few things he could thank Trey Sessions for was not contesting the divorce; of course, E.D. had legally boxed him in so magnificently, the poor fool was still looking befuddled most of the time.

This achievement meant all the more to Dylan with her at his side to share it with.

"Congratulations, darling," E.D. whispered when

it was over and the handshaking and backslapping commenced.

She was radiant in a winter-white suit with a diamond starburst brooch on the collar, which had been his wedding present to her. The gemstones didn't match the brilliance in her eyes, even without the tears of pride. As she lifted her face for a kiss, Dylan didn't care what protocol dictated or who was watching; having once believed he would never hear her say she loved him, he took advantage of any and every opportunity to kiss her breathless.

"All right, all right, put her down, caveman," Jonas Hunter teased as he reached them.

He'd flown down from the nation's capital to share in today, and Dylan would be forever grateful for all he'd done to shorten the duration of stress for E.D. and her daughter. With Geoffrey Post in particular, he'd probably saved countless other parents grief. Post had just been extradited to Colorado, with requests in South Dakota and Minnesota pending.

"I'm glad you could make it. You are coming back to the ranch for the party, aren't you?" Ivan Priestly had just left. Although recovering well from the heart attack, his doctor had him under strict orders not to push his luck. Dylan thought it would be a pity if another of their favorite people couldn't join them.

"Wouldn't miss it." Jonas bent to kiss E.D. on both cheeks. "My, Ms. Martel, this big lug seems to be agreeing with you."

"That's Mrs. Justiss to you, pal," Dylan interjected.

E.D. squeezed Jonas's arm before glancing around him with confusion. "I was sure I saw Alyx with you."

Jonas mimicked her search and frowned. "I think she said something about a phone call and vanished. Tell you what, while you two get through the reception line, I'll track her down and see you there."

Pushing his way through the crowd, Mac grinned at Dylan and his mother. "I saw the governor! You're important, sir."

Dylan was growing increasingly fond of the boy. "Well, thanks."

"I got his autograph," he added, patting the pocket of his blue suit jacket. "I'll bet I can get twenty bucks for it on e-bay."

That had E.D. groaning. "Say that a little louder, the people in the gallery haven't heard you."

More reserved, Dani edged forward. "I'll go on ahead and drive us to the ranch in my car if you think that's okay?"

Looking like a miniature version of her mother, but wearing purple, Dani kept her gaze low. She'd dreaded attending this ceremony for fear of stirring old gossip. Dylan had heard E.D. counseling her how to act last night. They were getting along well, although Dani had yet to attend a therapist's appointment without complaining. But she'd gotten her high school diploma, and was adjusting to college; that was why she'd got the promised new car.

"That would be good of you, Dani," E.D. said, kissing her left temple. "Drive safely, and do make sure he changes out of his new suit before he runs for the stable."

Dani rolled her eyes. "No kidding. I feel sorry for

Chris. That kid can be a pest." She cast Dylan a shy glance. "Congratulations, Judge."

"Thank you, Dani. And thank you for the help."

With a shy smile she left, too.

E.D. squeezed Dylan's arm. "Is it my imagination or is she developing a crush on Chris?"

"I think she could easily. But she's too young for him."

"Of course. I'm just saying he's a good man. At least her taste is improving."

"Oh, you noticed?"

Chuckling, E.D. rubbed his back. "Can we go to your chambers so you can get out of that robe and I can kiss you out of feeling like chopped liver?"

Back in his offices, Dylan wasted no time in closing the door and sweeping his wife into his arms. She felt like heaven against him, and her fragrance had him nuzzling the side of her neck to draw it deeper into his lungs.

"I think this is the second happiest day of my life," he murmured.

"I'm so proud of you."

"I'm humbled by you."

She had slowly but decisively begun to reduce her hours at the D.A.'s office. Emmett Garner had been steamed at first, then astonished when she told him that she had no desire to consider running for his seat in the next election—especially after championing the Reverend Betts fiasco and winning that case. Finally, if Dylan could bear more, she'd finally explained that curious remark spoken back in May when she'd left Alyx's office to confront Dani and her now ex.

"You're more important to me than an election," he'd said, concerned for her safety.

"So are you," she'd replied.

Even back then, she'd decided to put him and her children first.

Now, cupping her chin with his fingers, he claimed her lips for a long, adoring kiss. "Want to open that bottle of bubbly Paulie left us in my refrigerator?" he murmured, smiling into her eyes.

"Why don't you bring it back to the ranch and share it with the others?"

"I thought we'd stay here until they all went home."

"Aha. So that's why you wanted a couch in here, not just those leather chairs."

"That's one of the things I love about you—you're so quick. I'll go get the champagne."

E.D. caught his arm before he could take another step. "No champagne."

"That's the next thing I love about you," he murmured, his smile deepening. "You—" As she shook her head, he paused. "What am I missing?"

"The other reason why I might not drink any champagne," she said with a tender smile.

It came to Dylan with the same magical wonder as when he'd first set eyes on her. Dylan started to reach for her, held back, began to extend his fingers toward her flat belly, only to change his mind again and framed her face in his trembling hands.

"Really? A baby?"

Her eyes welling, E.D. nodded. "Surprise?"

That was the understatement of a lifetime.

He rained kisses over her face and then touched his lips to hers as though she were as fragile as gold thread. He'd believed a child of his own was never to be and now she was going to give him the greatest gift.

"My heart," he whispered. "Say it. Say it again."

She wrapped her arms around his neck. "I love you, I love you…I love you."

* * * * *

MEDITERRANEAN NIGHTS

Join the guests and crew of Alexandra's Dream,
*the newest luxury ship to set sail on the
romantic Mediterranean, as they experience
the glamorous world of cruising.*

*A new Harlequin continuity series
begins in June 2007 with*
FROM RUSSIA, WITH LOVE
by Ingrid Weaver

*Marina Artamova books a cabin on the luxurious
cruise ship* Alexandra's Dream, *when she finds
out that her orphaned nephew and his adoptive
father are aboard. She's determined to be reunited
with the boy...but the romantic ambience of the ship
and her undeniable attraction to a man she considers
her enemy are about to interfere with her quest!*

Turn the page for a sneak preview!

Piraeus, Greece

"THERE SHE IS, Stefan. *Alexandra's Dream*." David
Anderson squatted beside his new son and pointed at the
dark blue hull that towered above the pier. The cruise
ship was a majestic sight, twelve decks high and as long
as a city block. A circle of silver and gold stars, the logo
of the Liberty Cruise Line, gleamed from the swept-
back smokestack. Like some legendary sea creature
born for the water, the ship emanated power from every
sleek curve—even at rest it held the promise of motion.
"That's going to be our home for the next ten days."

The child beside him remained silent, his cheeks
working in and out as he sucked furiously on his thumb.
Hair so blond it appeared white ruffled against his
forehead in the harbor breeze. The baby-sweet scent
unique to the very young mingled with the tang of the sea.

"Ship," David said. "Uh, *parakhod*."

From beneath his bangs, Stefan looked at the
Alexandra's Dream. Although he didn't release his
thumb, the corners of his mouth tightened with the beginning of a smile.

David grinned. That was Stefan's first smile this afternoon, one of only two since they had left the orphanage yesterday. It was probably because of the boat—according to the orphanage staff, the boy loved boats, which was the main reason David had decided to book this cruise. Then again, there was a strong possibility the smile could have been a reaction to David's attempt at pocket-dictionary Russian. Whatever the cause, it was a good start.

The liaison from the adoption agency had claimed that Stefan had been taught some English, but David had yet to see evidence of it. David continued to speak, positive his son would understand his tone even if he couldn't grasp the words. "This is her maiden voyage. Her first trip, just like this is our first trip, and that makes it special." He motioned toward the stage that had been set up on the pier beneath the ship's bow. "That's why everyone's celebrating."

The ship's official christening ceremony had been held the day before and had been a closed affair, with only the cruise-line executives and VIP guests invited, but the stage hadn't yet been disassembled. Banners bearing the blue and white of the Greek flag of the ship's owner, as well as the Liberty circle-of-stars logo, draped the edges of the platform. In the center, a group of musicians and a dance troupe dressed in traditional white folk costumes performed for the benefit of the *Alexandra's Dream*'s first passengers. Their audience was in a festive mood, snapping their fingers in time to the music while the dancers twirled and wove through their steps.

David bobbed his head to the rhythm of the mandolins. They were playing a folk tune that seemed vaguely familiar, possibly from a movie he'd seen. He hummed a few notes. "Catchy melody, isn't it?"

Stefan turned his gaze on David. His eyes were a striking shade of blue, as cool and pale as a winter horizon and far too solemn for a child not yet five. Still, the smile that hovered at the corners of his mouth persisted. He moved his head with the music, mirroring David's motion.

David gave a silent cheer at the interaction. Hopefully, this cruise would provide countless opportunities for more. "Hey, good for you," he said. "Do you like the music?"

The child's eyes sparked. He withdrew his thumb with a pop. *"Moozika!"*

"Music. Right!" David held out his hand. "Come on, let's go closer so we can watch the dancers."

Stefan grasped David's hand quickly, as if he feared it would be withdrawn. In an instant his budding smile was replaced by a look close to panic.

Did he remember the car accident that had killed his parents? It would be a mercy if he didn't. As far as David knew, Stefan had never spoken of it to anyone. Whatever he had seen had made him run so far from the crash that the police hadn't found him until the next day. The event had traumatized him to the extent that he hadn't uttered a word until his fifth week at the orphanage. Even now he seldom talked.

David sat back on his heels and brushed the hair from Stefan's forehead. That solemn, too-old gaze locked with his, and for an instant, David felt as if he looked back in time at an image of himself thirty years ago.

He didn't need to speak the same language to understand exactly how this boy felt. He knew what it meant to be alone and powerless among strangers, trying to be brave and tough but wishing with every fiber of his being for a place to belong, to be safe, and most of all for someone to love him....

He knew in his heart he would be a good parent to Stefan. It was why he had never considered halting the adoption process after Ellie had left him. He hadn't balked when he'd learned of the recent claim by Stefan's spinster aunt, either; the absentee relative had shown up too late for her case to be considered. The adoption was meant to be. He and this child already shared a bond that went deeper than paperwork or legalities.

A seagull screeched overhead, making Stefan start and press closer to David.

"That's my boy," David murmured. He swallowed hard, struck by the simple truth of what he had just said.

That's my *boy*.

"I CAN'T BE PATIENT, RUDOLPH. I'm not going to stand by and watch my nephew get ripped from his country and his roots to live on the other side of the world."

Rudolph hissed out a slow breath. "Marina, I don't like the sound of that. What are you planning?"

"I'm going to talk some sense into this American kidnapper."

"No. Absolutely not. No offence, but diplomacy is not your strong suit."

"Diplomacy be damned. Their ship's due to sail at five o'clock."

"Then you wouldn't have an opportunity to speak with him even if his lawyer agreed to a meeting."

"I'll have ten days of opportunities, Rudolph, since I plan to be on board that ship."

* * * * *

*Follow Marina and David as they join forces
to uncover the reason behind little Stefan's
unusual silence, and the secret behind
the death of his parents....*

*Look for FROM RUSSIA, WITH LOVE
by Ingrid Weaver
in stores June 2007.*

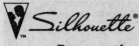

Silhouette®

Romantic
SUSPENSE

REQUEST YOUR FREE BOOKS!
2 FREE NOVELS PLUS 2 FREE GIFTS!

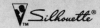

SPECIAL EDITION®
Life, Love and Family!

YES! Please send me 2 FREE Silhouette Special Edition® novels and my 2 FREE gifts. After receiving them, if I don't wish to receive any more books, I can return the shipping statement marked "cancel." If I don't cancel, I will receive 6 brand-new novels every month and be billed just $4.24 per book in the U.S., or $4.99 per book in Canada, plus 25¢ shipping and handling per book and applicable taxes, if any*. That's a savings of at least 15% off the cover price! I understand that accepting the 2 free books and gifts places me under no obligation to buy anything. I can always return a shipment and cancel at any time. Even if I never buy another book from Silhouette, the two free books and gifts are mine to keep forever.

235 SDN ÉEYU   335 SDN EEY6

Name	(PLEASE PRINT)
Address	Apt.
City	State/Prov.	Zip/Postal Code

Signature (if under 18, a parent or guardian must sign)

Mail to the Silhouette Reader Service™:
IN U.S.A.: P.O. Box 1867, Buffalo, NY 14240-1867
IN CANADA: P.O. Box 609, Fort Erie, Ontario L2A 5X3
Not valid to current Silhouette Special Edition subscribers.

Want to try two free books from another line?
Call 1-800-873-8635 or visit www.morefreebooks.com.

* Terms and prices subject to change without notice. NY residents add applicable sales tax. Canadian residents will be charged applicable provincial taxes and GST. This offer is limited to one order per household. All orders subject to approval. Credit or debit balances in a customer's account(s) may be offset by any other outstanding balance owed by or to the customer. Please allow 4 to 6 weeks for delivery.

Your Privacy: Silhouette is committed to protecting your privacy. Our Privacy Policy is available online at www.eHarlequin.com or upon request from the Reader Service. From time to time we make our lists of customers available to reputable firms who may have a product or service of interest to you. If you would prefer we not share your name and address, please check here. ☐

SSE07

nocturne™

IT'S TIME TO DISCOVER
THE RAINTREE TRILOGY...

There have always been those among us
who are more than human...

Don't miss the dramatic first book by
New York Times bestselling author

LINDA
HOWARD

RAINTREE:
Inferno

On sale May.

Raintree: Haunted by Linda Winstead Jones
Available June.

Raintree: Sanctuary by Beverly Barton
Available July.

HARLEQUIN

SuperRomance®

Acclaimed author
Brenda Novak
returns to Dundee, Idaho, with

COULDA BEEN A COWBOY

After gaining custody of his infant son,
professional athlete Tyson Garnier hopes to escape
the media and find some privacy in Dundee, Idaho.
He also finds Dakota Brown. But is she ready for the
potential drama that comes with him?

Also watch for:

BLAME IT ON THE DOG by Amy Frazier
(Singles...with Kids)

HIS PERFECT WOMAN by Kay Stockham

DAD FOR LIFE by Helen Brenna
(A Little Secret)

MR. IRRESISTIBLE by Karina Bliss

WANTED MAN by Ellen K. Hartman

Available June 2007 wherever Harlequin books are sold!

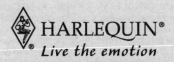

HARLEQUIN®
Live the emotion

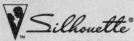

COMING NEXT MONTH

SSECNM0507